His thum

mouth.

Entranced, Kitt

and taste his skin. Salt. Warmth. Ridged thumbprint, as uniquely his as his eyes still on her. Jack made a sound deep in his throat and it reverberated within her own chest. The tip of his thumb slid between her lips, into her mouth.

Oh, God, this was Jack, inside her, filling her senses with just that small piece of flesh. She closed her lips around him. She closed her eyes and felt only the pleasure of his touch there, on the thin membrane of the inside of her lip, between her teeth like the most luscious fruit she'd ever tasted.

Dear Reader

This story is about dreams. Jack's dream is about sex...well, what else would a true playboy dream about? Kitty's dream is about love, and her longings and her hopelessness are based on every teenage crush I ever had. (Yeah, I had a lot of them.) And their story is set in the movie theatre, where we watch the stars acting out all of our fantasies.

This story is about my dream, too. I'd wanted to write romance ever since I was a teenager, and I hid myself in our local library reading all the Mills & Boon® romances I could get my hands on. I loved the spirited characters, the fun world-view, and of course the sexy stories. *Mumble* years and three rejected manuscripts later, Jack and Kitty's story finalled in the Romance Writers of America's Golden Heart contest, and four months later I got the call telling me that my story was going to be published. Dreams do come true. This book is the proof.

If you want to stay with the fantasy a little longer, look out for BEING A BAD GIRL, where Jack's friend Oz discovers what happens when you mix a Harley and a sexy bartender.

I love to hear from readers—contact me via my website, www.julie-cohen.com, or write to me at Harlequin Mills & Boon, Eton House, 18-24 Paradise Road, Richmond, Surrey, TW9 1SR, UK.

Julie Cohen

Look out for BEING A BAD GIRL,
the sequel to FEATURED ATTRACTION,
available in April in Modern Extra.

FEATURED ATTRACTION

Julie Cohen

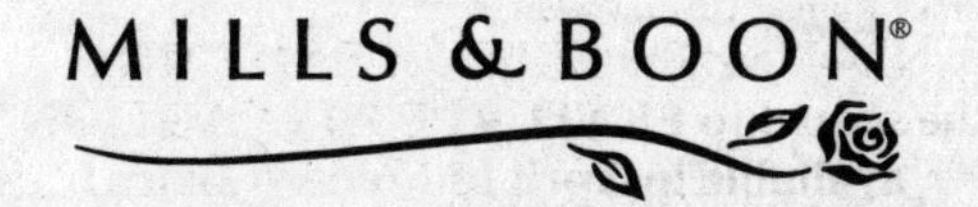

First published in Great Britain 2006
Harlequin Mills & Boon Limited,
Eton House, 18-24 Paradise Road, Richmond, Surrey TW9 1SR

ISBN 0 263 84984 8

Set in Times Roman 10¼ on 12 pt.
171-0306-65413

Printed and bound in Spain
by Litografia Rosés S.A., Barcelona

To the eHarlequin Writing Romance Community: the Struggling Writers, the Spaketeers, the Mouse and Pen special ops team, the SubCare Borg. If I hadn't spent so much time procrastinating with all of you, it would have taken a lot longer.

PROLOGUE

JACK TAYLOR was making love with the most beautiful woman in the world.

He couldn't see her, but Jack didn't need to. His hands caressed her silky skin and found it flawless. His fingers touched the hollow of her back, the delicate ridges of her spine. He stroked upwards, exploring her perfect curves of waist and ribs. When he took her breasts in his hands she gasped and then moaned as he teased her taut nipples.

The sound of her voice wordlessly describing her pleasure warmed the blood in his veins, sent his heart throbbing faster, matching the racing pulse that he could feel beneath the curve of her breast.

He had never been this turned on before. Ever.

And Jack Taylor had had a lot of experience with being turned on.

His lover turned her face toward him and he felt her soft hair brush his face. He tasted her mouth. Her lips and tongue were sweet, as if she'd been licking candy, but Jack knew that this taste was a part of her. As much a part of her as her hair, her voice and her body. And the feeling she gave him was part of her, too. All of it was infinitely, excitingly, astoundingly sweet.

"I want you now," she whispered. Heat shivered down his body again.

"I want you more than I've ever wanted anyone. Anything." He spoke it aloud, and knew it was the truest thing he'd ever said.

And then her hand was on him, guiding him into her, and for Jack the darkness was filled with an ecstasy that was brighter than light.

She took his hand and brought it to her mouth. He traced her smile with his fingers and while she began to move beneath him, he began to move inside her. Exquisitely slowly, so perfect and arousing that Jack lost any sense of time. He caught her hand in his and laid it on his own smile, nibbling on each of her fingers.

There was nothing besides the two of them. Their movements quickened, and he plunged still deeper within her. God, it felt so good. The best in his life. He felt her shudder around him, felt his own climax building. There was only one thing he needed before he could let himself go over the edge, and that was—

"Jack!" she cried out, and the rich honey of her voice flooded his veins. Her voice in his ears, his body joined with hers, his mind and his heart overwhelmed like never before, Jack shouted out his own release and, with it, he suddenly saw her eyes.

Green. The green of springtime and summer. The green of life and eternal promise. They looked into his, and wrung from him a final, shattering wave of ecstasy.

And then it all went black.

Jack awoke panting. He ran a hand through his perspiration-soaked hair and sat up, damp sheets twisted around his waist.

"Wow," he said.

It wasn't quite dark. He could see the stars through his open bedroom window and the whiteness of the sheets around him. Still, he had to reach out and feel the bed beside him to make sure that it was cold and empty.

He disentangled himself from the bedding and went down the hall to the bathroom. The light in there was harsh, and as

Jack splashed his face with cold water the mirror starkly reflected every detail. His cheeks were flushed, his eyes hooded and pupils dilated, a satisfied smile lifting the corners of his lips.

He looked like a man who'd had the best sex in the history of sex.

Which, in a way, he had.

Jack's smile broadened. And then he watched it slowly melt away.

He'd had the most intense sexual experience of his entire life…and it had been a dream?

Jack turned abruptly and loped down the stairs. He walked naked into his dark living room. From touch and from memory he lifted scratchy handfuls of kindling and paper from the box on the floor and layered them in the fireplace. He stacked wood on top of the pile and lit it all with the long stroke of a match.

Jack watched as the fire licked at the kindling and curled around the logs. He remembered the taste of his dream lover and how her limbs had twined around him. The heat in their touching bodies.

He waited until the fire was raging before he stood and crossed the orange-lit room to his desk. Without looking, he found the palm-sized book in the top drawer. He knelt with it in front of the fire.

He licked his lips and thought he could still taste her sweetness. But of course he couldn't. She was a fantasy. And yet somehow more real than anything or anyone he'd ever experienced.

One by one, Jack Taylor tore the pages out of his address book and fed the names and telephone numbers of the women he knew to the flames.

CHAPTER ONE

SOMETIMES the real world just sucks.

Kitty Giroux Clifford looked at the man sitting across from her, straight in the eye, and asked, "So, how much will you give me for my Mercedes?"

The used-car dealer put one finger on his pudgy chin and hesitated. "It's got a lot of miles on it for last year's model. And there's not much call for convertibles here in Maine. Winter's too rough."

Kitty pulled herself up taller in her chair. She needed every penny she could get for the car to pay her debts and keep her business going, but she was not going to appear desperate.

Even though she was. And the dealer knew it. People didn't trade in their Mercedes for cash unless they were going down in the world.

"Maybe there's more call for convertibles at the dealership in Scarborough," she said. She pulled down the jacket of her designer suit and made as if to stand, and was rewarded by the dealer holding up his hands to stop her.

"Hold on, Ms. Clifford," he said. "I'm sure we can come to an arrangement."

Victory.

She smiled, and at that moment felt her handbag vibrate. Her heart leapt, as it did every time her cell rang. *This could be it.*

"Excuse me," she said, and pulled her phone out of her bag.

Big surprise—it was her mother's number on the phone and not the business deal of the century. Seemed as if Kitty would be used to being let down by now.

"I'm sorry, I have to take this," she said, anyway. It couldn't hurt if the car dealer thought her time was valuable. She rose and pressed the answer button as she walked out the door and into the parking lot. "Katherine Clifford."

"Kitty!" Her mother's voice was high-pitched and excited. "You just got a call from someone who wants you for a job! And guess where?"

Kitty's calmed-down pulse sped up again. She'd started her interior design business here in Maine six months ago, and this was the first bit of interest she'd had.

"It's work? Where?"

"Oh, you'll love it. He's bought the Delphi Theater, on Congress Street. He's restoring it."

"Yes!" Kitty practically shouted it. She spun around and punched the air.

The Delphi Theater was the most elegant building in Portland. She'd never been a movie fan, but Kitty had loved the Delphi ever since she'd been a little girl. It looked like a shabby palace. The sort of place where you'd find a slightly tarnished Prince Charming.

Of course, she'd grown out of fantasies like that. But ever since she'd moved back home, she'd stopped to admire the now-derelict cinema whenever she passed it. Even years of neglect hadn't been able to destroy its art deco lines. Restoring it was an interior designer's dream come true.

Maybe her luck was getting better, at last.

"He said he'd be at the theater this afternoon, if you could come by," her mother said. "And I've written down his number, if you want to call him."

Kitty skipped in her high heels. "Mom, this is great! What's his name?"

"Taylor."

She stopped dead, halfway across the parking lot.

Jack Taylor always loved the movies.

It couldn't be.

"What?"

"Taylor. That's his name."

Everything, suddenly, felt very brittle. Kitty spoke into the phone carefully. "What's his first name?"

"I didn't catch it. He sounded very nice."

This was her first real chance since her divorce and starting her new business. And her client might be—

"How do you spell Taylor, Mom?"

"I wrote it down as T-a-i-l-o—"

"Are you sure it's not T-a-y?"

A pause at the other end of the line. "Well, it sounded like it was spelled with an 'i' to me."

How on earth had her mother survived for thirty years as a receptionist at a vet's office? Maybe dogs didn't mind it if you misspelled their names.

"Tailor. Taylor. Mom, they sound exactly the same."

"Kitty. It doesn't matter, does it? It's exactly the job you've been waiting for."

Yes. It was her dream job.

But Jack Taylor was her worst nightmare.

He was Kitty's high-school crush. The person who'd trampled on her heart and humiliated her in front of the entire school at her junior prom. The one person in the world she never, ever wanted to see again.

She'd been back in her hometown for six months without running into Jack Taylor. She'd thought maybe he'd left. Portland was a small city. It would never hold enough women to keep Jack happy.

Forget Portland. The whole world probably didn't hold

enough women to keep Jack happy. The man went through girlfriends like most people went through Kleenex.

That was, if Jack was still the same as he'd been in high school. But why would he change? He was rich, and gorgeous, and charming enough that females fell in love with him on sight.

Kitty certainly had, thirteen years ago.

"Sweetheart? Do you want his number? You can ask him how he spells his name yourself."

Real world. Stay in the real world, Kitty. She realized that she was standing in the middle of the lot, twisting a lock of her red hair tightly around one of her fingers and holding the phone in a death grip to her ear, while the dealer watched her through the window. And before that, he'd probably seen her dancing around and punching the air.

But what the car dealer thought didn't matter now. If she had work, she could keep her car. She could talk with the bank, and rearrange her loan payments, and—

She wasn't going down in the world, after all.

"Mom, my day planner's in the car. I'll call you back in a minute and get Mr. Taylor's number, okay? I need to talk with someone first."

Kitty shoved her phone back into her handbag and walked into the office. The dealer didn't bother to stand when she entered.

"I've decided not to sell my car, Mr. Dawson," she said, scooping her keys from the desk. "Thank you for your time."

The surprised look on his jowly face was enough to make her giggle as she left. Her luck was definitely changing. The Delphi. Wow.

Suddenly very anxious to call her mother back, Kitty hurried across the parking lot again to her convertible. She needed this job. Not only because of the money—she needed it for herself. She'd been successful in California, but she'd failed at her marriage to Sam. Coming back to Maine was supposed to be a whole big self-renewal thing, to prove she could be a success on her own, but so far it hadn't worked, and her savings had all but disappeared.

If she could get this job right, everything would finally fall into place. She knew it. A movie theater was high profile. A real showcase for her talent. It would lead to more work.

By the time she reached her convertible, her giggle had turned into a full-size grin. She reached for her handbag to unzip it, and found it was already unzipped. Her grin fading, Kitty stuck her hand inside her bag.

Empty.

"Oh, no." She looked back over the parking lot. Her wallet, her car keys, a powder compact, six or seven pencils, a lipstick, a brush and her sleek, expensive, high-tech silver cell phone all lay on the pavement in a trail behind her.

She stepped forward to pick up her stuff, and jumped back against her convertible when a horn blared in her ears.

Kitty watched as a red Lexus with a sign on its windshield saying "Take Me For A Test Drive!" drove straight over her phone. She heard a crunch of plastic.

"Hey!" she yelled, waving her empty handbag at the Lexus. "You killed my phone, you jerk!" She ran after the car for a few steps. It didn't stop. The driver didn't even glance in his rearview mirror, as far as she could tell.

"Hope you buy the car and get ripped off," she muttered as she stooped and collected her wallet and other belongings, thankfully undamaged. She prodded what had once been her phone with the toe of her ivory shoe. It was a pile of sleek silver smithereens.

Kitty straightened. Okay, her phone was dead. And she couldn't afford to replace it. But she had other things to focus on right now. Such as getting this Delphi contract and doing a fantastic job.

Her mother had said she could just go by the Delphi and talk with this guy, Tailor, Taylor, whoever he was. So she'd do that.

These days, she carried her portfolio with her everywhere, in case she got a call. She was dressed for business already, wearing her best designer suit in ivory silk, to impress the car dealer. She'd fought with her hair for a good hour this morning and won the victory, more or less. She looked as good as she was going to look.

If Kitty had learned one thing in her life, it was that appearances were important. An interior designer had to look tasteful. Even more importantly for business, she had to look successful—wear the right clothes, drive the right car. Winners looked like winners.

That was the idea, anyway. It hadn't always worked for her, so far. Her expensive car and her designer clothes hadn't helped her keep her marriage going, or gotten her any work yet in Maine.

But this time, Kitty vowed to herself as she got into her Mercedes and started the ignition, she was going to be a winner. Everything was going to go right.

And if her new client was Jack Taylor, she would just...deal with it.

But it wouldn't be Jack. There were a hundred Taylors and Tailors in the phone book. What were the chances that her new client was her high-school crush?

Even Kitty's luck couldn't be that bad.

"Jack, have you considered the possibility that you're embarking on this elaborate building scheme to distract yourself from your sexual frustration?" Oz asked.

With a grunt, Jack ripped the last corner of the mouldering carpet from the floor.

"You're wrong, Oz. For one thing, I've wanted to do this for years, you know that. Remember how we always drove by this place and imagined what it must've been like when it was new?"

"*You* always imagined. I always thought, Man, what a dump."

Jack ignored his friend. "And remember my ambitions in our high-school yearbook? 'To own my own cinema, and make my life like a movie'? I've fulfilled the first part. And it's only taken me ten years." He pushed the massive roll of carpet forward against the wall, exposing the full extent of the wooden parquet flooring underneath. "If someone will make a film about fighting with smelly carpets, I'll have fulfilled the second part, too. What do you think—*Rocky VI: Rocky Hits the Carpet*?"

"That one would go straight to video." Oz didn't look up from where he knelt studying the floor, his blond hair dangling in front of his eyes.

"Another thing. 'Sexual frustration' implies that I can't get sex. And I can get sex. In fact, I ran into Sally McKenna last night, and she seemed very interested in reliving old times with me."

"Sally wants to sleep with you again? And you turned her down? Did you give her my number?"

"Get your own girlfriends, Oz. The point is, if I chose to have sex, I could. But I'm choosing not to. Until the right time."

Oz spread his big hand over the parquet tiles and pushed. "I hope your working parts are holding out better under neglect than this floor has. How long has it been since you chose the path of righteous chastity? A year?"

"Eleven months, six days and eight hours. Approximately." With a mighty heave, Jack wrestled the roll of carpet upright. "And there's nothing wrong with my working parts."

"It's good you're so certain of that, because the purchase of this immense architectural erection could be interpreted as a compensatory response to inadequacies in your physical performance."

Jack laughed, wiping sweat from his forehead and pushing

his dark hair back. "Okay, Dr. Strummer, you can quit using those degrees in psychology on me. I bought the Delphi Theater because I wanted it. It has nothing to do with my penis."

Oz finally looked up at Jack. He opened his mouth to respond, but instead broke into a huge grin. "You might say so, but it doesn't take a Ph.D. in psychology to understand the significance of *that.*"

He pointed over Jack's shoulder to the roll of carpet that towered above him. Jack turned in time to see the roll sag in the middle and slowly topple over to lie limply on the floor.

He threw back his head and laughed. "No way, Oz," he said, walking across the dusty floor toward his friend. "That did not mean a thing. I have absolutely no trouble getting a ha—aaaaaaagh!"

The floor opened up underneath Jack's feet and he came crashing down into darkness. He lay, winded, on his back, and saw Oz's shaggy blond head appear above him.

"Hey, buddy, you okay down there?"

"Yeah. Yeah, just surprised." Jack sat up and ran his hand through his hair, dislodging dust and splinters.

"I think you fell through a trapdoor," Oz said. "Looks like your weight ripped out the hinges and it just fell in."

"So this is how you get to the basement." Jack looked around; he was about seven feet below the floor. He'd landed on a heap of dirty rags that had broken his fall. The speckled light, filtered through flakes of plaster and dust motes, showed him that the space extended around him in all directions.

Oz tested the floor with his foot and, satisfied that it was safe, sat down near the lip of the trapdoor. "I'm sure I don't need to mention the symbolism of your falling down a hole."

"Ha, ha. Very funny. Will you help me out of here?"

"Not yet. I'm glad I've got you trapped, Jack, because I want to tell you seriously that I'm worried about you. The pickup king has gone eleven months without sex? It isn't like you. And all because of some random dream."

"It wasn't any dream. It was the best dream of my life. It made me realize that I was wasting my time jumping from one woman to another. Sex in that dream was the most incredible thing I've ever experienced. And I don't see the point in having sex until it can be that way for real."

"Jack, dreams are fantasy. Reality can never be as good. It's the nature of dreams."

"No. Not this dream. It'll happen. I know it." Jack pulled a long splinter of wood from his T-shirt. "Did you know my grandmother was a stage psychic? She used to tell the future for a living. It probably runs in the family."

Oz snorted. "You don't believe in that crap, do you?"

"Hey, that's my grandmother you're insulting. I should fight you."

"Okay," Oz said, in his let's-be-reasonable psychologist's voice. "Let's grant that you had some amazing dream that showed you the true extent of how great sex can be. And that instead of being the product of your oversexed and very imaginative mind, it has some basis in objective reality. Even if all of that is true, how will you know when you meet the woman you'll be having this incredible sex with?"

"I'll know."

"How?"

"I just will. Have you seen *The End of the Affair*? Julianne Moore and Ralph Fiennes look at each other and from that moment it's only a matter of time before they tear each other's clothes off. Like that."

Oz threw his hands up in frustration. "This is why I'm worried about you, Jack. You've never committed to anything or anyone in your life. You've skated through everything you've done and come out the other side without so much as a bruise. Now you're suddenly taking on a huge commitment with this cinema. And you've given up a very active and, frankly, enviable sex life because of a dream. Are you really ready to commit to this dream woman, if you ever do find her?"

"Whoa. One step at a time, big guy. I want to find her, and have sex with her. Let's leave the 'c' word out of it right now."

Oz shook his head. "Jack, have you ever considered that you want to make your life like a movie because movies only last for two hours?"

"*Gone With the Wind* lasted over three and a half hours. And don't even get me talking about *The Lord of the Rings*."

"You know what I mean. Movies aren't messy, like reality. You watch them, you walk away. There's no risk involved, no emotional investment. Isn't that why you want to make your life like them?"

Jack shrugged. "And your point is?"

"How long have you ever stuck with anything? A job, a project, a woman? And now suddenly you're taking all of this on. It's a commitment, whether you know it or not. Even the dream woman. I wonder whether you're ready for it."

"Stop psychologizing me, Oscar. I can have an attention span of more than two hours. I'll prove it to you." He stretched his hand up toward Oz. "I promise you that within a year the Delphi Theater will be a fully functioning, beautiful cinema. And I will have had the best sex of my life. And I'm willing to do whatever it takes to make both of those things happen."

Oz nodded and extended his hand down the hole to shake Jack's.

"So now will you help me up?"

Oz's hand stopped moving. "Yeah, just a second." He pulled out of Jack's grip and disappeared.

"Oz? Oz!" There was a pile of bricks and rubble near Jack's feet; he stepped up on it, but still couldn't see over the edge of the hole. He could hear his friend's footsteps walking away, and a door opening.

"Hello. Are you the new owner?" A feminine voice reached his ears.

Something went funny in Jack's chest. A tightening, a jolt. He stopped trying to look out of the hole. He stood very still and listened.

"No, he's stuck in a symbolic hole at the moment. Come in."

"I'm Katherine Clifford, the interior designer. I'm looking for a Mr. Taylor?"

The interior designer he'd picked out of the phone book. Her voice seemed so familiar. The upward lilt at the end of the sentence, something about how she said his name.

Jack felt his heartbeat speed up and his hands become damp with perspiration. He tensed every muscle in his body, trying to catch what it was about her voice that called to him, sang to him, made him want to jump the seven feet out of the hole he was in.

Oz was speaking. "Well, as you can see, you've got your work cut out for you here." Jack heard them stop walking. "Hey, I know you, don't I? Aren't you from around here? I'm Oscar Strummer."

"Oh!" There was a faint breathiness there, a little huskiness in her voice, that made Jack's mouth go dry. "You're Oscar Strummer? Oz?"

"That's right."

"So—um, hold on. Can you just clarify—? I mean, the message I received was from a Mr. Taylor, spelled T-a-i-l-o-r."

"Nope. T-a-y-l-o-r. First name Jack. He's the owner. I'm just the idiot friend who said he'd help out in his spare time. So how do I know you, Katherine?"

"Yes, Katherine, how do I know you?" Jack breathed, down in the darkness.

Had they met eleven months ago, one night in his sleep?

"Jack Taylor owns the Delphi?" There was a little pause. "We went to high school together," he heard Katherine say.

"You were both the year ahead of me. I didn't recognize you when I came in, you're much taller than you were in school."

"You mean I used to be a short, skinny geek," Oz said, laughing. "I got my growth spurt late. I recognized you as soon as I saw your hair. The name Katherine Clifford didn't ring a bell, though."

She'd gone to high school with him and Oz. That was why he recognized her voice. He stepped forward, trying to hear better, and knocked a brick off the pile he was standing on, which meant he missed half of her reply to Oz.

"—came back to Portland about six months ago to start my own business. And, yeah, people tend to remember my hair." She laughed, and Jack broke out in a sweat.

He swallowed and tried to calm himself. They'd met in high school, not in his dream. It was because he'd been talking about the dream that his body was reacting so extremely. And delayed adrenaline from his fall.

If there were such a thing as delayed adrenaline.

He had to get out of this basement. Jack looked around him again. By now, his eyes had adjusted to the light and he could see farther. About five feet from him were some large objects covered with gray sheets. Above his head, he heard Oz asking the woman questions, what she'd been doing since high school, if she still had family in the area, things like that. He couldn't concentrate on her replies; what he heard instead was her voice, sweet and throaty, like a feather tickling his ear with playful, erotic strokes.

And Oz, that rat, that handsome *single* rat, had her undivided attention.

Jack pulled the sheet off the nearest object: a shabby velvet-covered chair. He dragged it over the rubble to underneath the trapdoor.

Who was she? He couldn't remember any Katherines from high school. What was it about her hair?

She laughed again, and there was nothing delayed about the adrenaline rush he felt when he heard her. Jack scrambled onto the chair, seized the edge of the opening and hurled himself up onto the floor. He slid a few feet on the wooden tiles, then sprang to his feet and ran. Heart pounding, Jake dashed across the foyer to where Oz stood, looking down at a slender woman who was facing away from Jack. She had luxurious hair the color of blazing autumn leaves, loosely pulled back to her nape. It looked familiar.

He skidded to a stop beside her and held out his hand. "Hi, I'm Jack."

It seemed like forever until she turned around. Jack saw her as if she were moving in slow motion—delicate neck and chin; fine, straight nose; full pink mouth; pale skin. And that bright red hair.

He knew her all right.

She was probably the only person in the world who'd ever hated him.

CHAPTER TWO

"KITTY GIROUX?" Jack gasped.

"My name is Katherine Clifford now," she corrected. Her eyes flashed over his face before dropping to his clothes. "You really have been in a hole."

Jack looked down at himself. He was covered with gray dust and streaks of brown dirt, and his jeans had a jagged tear in one knee. He brushed his hands down his front and a small cloud formed in the air.

Jack coughed, swallowed, looked at Kitty and attempted to put some of his usual trademark charm into his reply. "Yeah, I always like to make a dramatic entrance."

"I see." Her voice seemed to have changed; maybe because he was closer to her now. That warmth, that honey-edged sexiness, was gone. Instead, her words were dry and clipped.

"Well, Mr. Taylor, I've brought some examples of my work that you may want to look through before we discuss your needs for the Delphi." He saw for the first time that she wore a tailored skirt and jacket in creamy ivory and carried a large leather portfolio.

"Jack. Call me Jack, please. We went to high school together, remember?" He held out his hand again for her to shake.

Her fingers were cold and allowed only the briefest contact before she withdrew them. "I remember. Do you have a desk or a table where I can lay out my portfolio?"

This did not sound like the woman who had been talking with Oz minutes before. *Invasion of the Body Snatchers,* he thought, and then instantly dismissed it. In real life, responsive, laughing, sexy women didn't instantaneously get taken over by distant, businesslike aliens. It was much more likely that, after eleven months, six days, eight hours and twenty minutes, Jack Taylor had lost the knack for making women swoon at his feet.

Either that, or she was still mad at him for what had happened in high school. But prom night had been ten years ago, right?

Jack shoved his hand, which was tingling strangely from the small, chilly contact, into the back pocket of his jeans.

"Actually, I think it would be better to show you around first," he said. "The place needs a lot of plain old renovation before we start decorating it, but I want to get a designer involved as soon as possible to see what we can preserve of the period features. If you don't run screaming out into the street, I'll assume you want the job."

The smallest of smiles. Even that was a knockout. Man, it could be because he hadn't touched a woman in nearly a year, but to his mind Kitty Giroux was the most beautiful woman he had seen...well, maybe ever, in real life.

Her hair, for one thing. It was even more vivid than he remembered. Its color, of course: rich, fiery, gleaming with warmth. But more than that, it seemed to have a life of its own. It had escaped the clips that held it back, and curled in tendrils around her face, near the shells of her ears and down the back of her white neck.

Her body, for another. She'd been cute in high school, but she'd definitely grown up since then. Her suit was businesslike, but still fit every curve of her as if it were snuggling up for a good hug. She had delicate shoulders and, from what he could see peeking out between the lapels of her jacket, an exquisite collarbone, dusted with freckles. Full breasts and a narrow waist that curved out into hips a man could drool over. Long, long, movie-star legs, ending in ivory high-heeled shoes.

She looked like Nicole Kidman, he thought, only less ethereal, more luscious. Fuller in the lips, less transparent in the skin.

And nobody else, not even a film star, could have hair so vibrant. He wanted to sink his fingers into it, bury his face in it and inhale its perfume. He could smell its vanilla and cinnamon scent now. He pictured it on his naked chest, spread out across his skin, springing against his fingers, every curl a caress. It would be easy to reach out now and let that strand by her ear entwine itself around his finger…

"That portfolio looks heavy. Let me take it for you, Kitty." Oz's voice broke Jack's reverie.

Of course! Politeness! And Oz, considerate, handsome, polite, *single* Oz, whom Jack had just told to get his own girlfriend, had thought of it first.

Jack's charm had definitely gone rusty.

"Thank you." Kitty was all gracious smiles for Oz as she handed over her leather case.

"So." Jack's voice sounded unsteady to his own ears; he cleared his throat and started again. He held out his arm as if he were presenting the room to Kitty.

"So. The Delphi Theater. Built in 1926, originally as a music hall. It was converted to a cinema in the thirties and showed films until it closed in 1996. From 1999 it was Portland's largest X-rated movie house. I've searched through the whole building looking for relics of that time, but I haven't found any yet."

Oz chuckled at this. Kitty stayed silent. Jack carried on anyway, feeling slightly foolish.

"This is the lobby; you can see the original art deco detailing still on the walls and ceiling. They tell me all the black stains were caused by a minor fire they had last year. Some kids were having a party that got out of control. You should have seen the bags of empty beer cans Oz and I carried out of here when I first bought the place."

He walked across the spacious, high-ceilinged room, gesturing at the features he pointed out to Kitty as she followed him. The electric light made the dark wooden panelling on the walls look slightly yellow.

"This is the box office, and the concession stand is over here." He ran a finger over the dusty blue tiles of the concession counter. "The original tiling is mostly intact, though some of it will need replacing. Men's room over there on the other side of the room, and ladies' next to it. The ladies' is a real powder room, with a big mirror and space for seats. And of course, in the middle of the lobby there's the broken trapdoor in the floor. Which I've been examining closely, as you know."

Jack looked at Kitty's face. Still impassive, and she wouldn't meet his gaze. Though what Oz was thinking was plain for any idiot to see. The big lug was practically slobbering.

He led them to a set of dark wooden double doors. They opened to a short, semi-lit corridor, ending in another set of doors. "This is the light trap. It stops light from coming in with the customers and spoiling the film. There's a similar vestibule at the front doors of the cinema, though I think that's to keep cold air from coming into the lobby in the winter."

He opened the second set of doors and ushered them both into the musty darkness. "And this is the real heart of the Delphi," he said.

Anticipation, excitement, a showman's pride in spectacle made him smile to himself as he flicked on the lights. Maybe Kitty Giroux wasn't impressed with him, but she had to be impressed with *this*.

She gasped.

Row after row of chairs created an intricate pattern like the scales of a red velvet fish. They sloped down to the stage, a huge white screen flanked by dazzling gold pillars. Gold leaves, gold fruit, gold flowers, gold fire wreathed the walls, climbing a gilded trellis up the mahogany-stained walls to a ceiling of midnight-blue, painted with thousands and thousands of silver stars.

A temple of illusion. A palace of visions. The very, very best thing in the world.

"It's gorgeous." That honeyed note was back in her voice.

Jack examined her face, looking for wonder. And it was there. Her lush lips parted themselves. Her eyes were huge, luminous, taking in everything at once. She stepped forward and ran her fingertips over the velvet back of a chair. Then ran the backs of her fingers over the next chair.

Watching her, Jack saw the sensuality in her touch, saw how her hand lingered on the soft fabric—the place where hundreds of heads had rested, losing themselves to a fantasy.

He could imagine how those fingertips would touch him, how they would trail down his own face, down his body, caress with one thumb, as she was doing to the velvet in front of her now.

He couldn't help it. He touched her arm just above the elbow and spoke quietly into her ear. "Doesn't it make you feel like your dreams can come true?"

Kitty stiffened. She sidestepped, pulling her arm out of his grip. "Of course," she said, her voice again pure business, "it needs lots of work."

With those words the illusion shattered. Once again, Jack could see the rips in the velvet upholstery of the chairs. The disturbing stains. How the silver screen was slashed; the outbreak of graffiti in the corner like acne on a teenager. Golden fruit drooped from the walls, stalks broken. He could smell the mildewed breath of the place and could hear the scratching behind the golden pillars that probably meant mice, or worse.

He could see Kitty saw all of that and more.

Jack took a deep breath, and when he let it out he was just very, very tired. This place wasn't a movie; it was reality. He had lots of work to do. He was going to have to spend lots of money, and sweat and probably blood, in order to do it.

And while Kitty Giroux was absolutely stunning and beautiful, he'd been wrong. She wasn't the woman he had dreamed about. She was someone he'd been friends with in high school—and they hadn't even been friends by the end of his senior year.

He was just sexually frustrated. As Oz had said.

"Yeah," he said. "Lots of work. So are you interested in the job, Kitty?"

"I prefer to be called Katherine now."

She pushed the wooden doors open and walked back into the lobby, her heels clicking on the dusty parquet floor. Jack and Oz followed her.

"So I assume you want to restore the place as far as possible, and to choose furniture and fittings that will complement what's already here," she said.

Jack nodded. He was still smarting from her rebuff, but that shouldn't matter anyway. If she wasn't the woman in his dream, he couldn't get involved with her, no matter how tempting she was. And thinking about restoring the Delphi, as always, got him enthusiastic.

"I want to bring it back to its original glory, but with modern comfort and technology," he said.

"Exactly. So I'll have to do a lot of research and sourcing as well as design. We'll have to commission quite a few bespoke items, I imagine. It will be a real challenge, but should produce spectacular results. If you're really committed, that is. And willing to spend the cash."

"I'm more than committed. And I've got the cash."

She smiled again, a little wider than before. "Well, then, Mr. Taylor, I'd be glad to take the job."

"Great!" Jack grinned. Yeah, so he was disappointed that Kitty wasn't the one he'd dreamed about. But even though she didn't seem to like him, she saw the potential in the Delphi. And she was going to help him achieve it. They could be friends again.

He held out his hand for her to shake. "I'm looking forward to working with you. And, please, call me Jack."

Kitty took his hand and this time her skin was warmer. Jack wrapped his hand round hers and squeezed, fully savoring the feeling of her flesh against his. He actually drew her a little bit closer—hey, it couldn't hurt if he wasn't going to take it any further, right? At least their business relationship was going to be a good one.

Then Kitty, smiling, looked directly into his eyes for the first time.

Jack froze, struck with something as powerful as a bolt of lightning. His hearing, his thoughts, the floor beneath his feet all shattered away and his entire being focused on the pair of eyes before him.

Her eyes were green. The green of springtime and summer. The green of life and eternal promise.

It was her.

It was a zap, a spark, a shock that caught his breath in his throat and seized his heart. He had a dim sense of each hair on his body shivering upright, charged with energy.

"Jack."

Her rich voice lilted his name, and that was his dream, too. With it, the electricity of the lightning bolt that had struck him turned into pure heat.

He wanted her. More than that: he needed her, with an urgency he'd never felt before, not in a lifetime of playing around.

He dragged a breath into his lungs. Every atom of it was perfumed with her hair and her skin. His crotch swelled into instant, throbbing hardness.

His mouth hungered to devour hers, every inch of his skin craved hers pressed against it, sliding together, slick with sweat and heat. Her hand in his trembled, though maybe it was his own hand that shook; he couldn't be sure of anything except for this desire.

Jack's eyes didn't waver from hers, but they looked deeper. He saw her pupils dilate and her eyes widen with knowledge.

She wanted him, too.

He stepped toward her, a tantalizing few inches from her body now, and bent his head toward hers. His only thoughts were to kiss her. To pick her up, wrap her around him. To taste her, anywhere and everywhere. Her mouth parted and she sighed softly. Another moment, another movement, and he would be in heaven.

Then it was gone.

Kitty snatched her hand from his and skittered back several steps on her high heels. "I—" He heard her gulp in a breath. "I've got to go."

"Go?"

"Yes, I'm—I've got something else to do." She caught her bottom lip between her teeth, and Jack felt even weaker in the knees. "I mean," she said, "I've got another meeting. For work. You know. But I'm wicked excited to be working on this job, I mean this building is totally awesome, and it'll be...um..."

Kitty's words were rapid, breathless, but now she paused. Her delicate eyebrows contracted together, and she rubbed her hand across her forehead. "Good. Okay, see you later." Abruptly, she turned and headed for the door.

Jack watched her go, not sure if it was his head that was spinning or if his cinema had suddenly turned into a carousel.

"Kitty? You forgot your portfolio."

Oz was still here? Jack's friend loped after Jack's dream woman and held out her leather case.

"Oh! Thank you." She took it, hugged it to her chest, and then turned toward Jack. He was still rooted to the spot, but his eyes desperately sought out hers. She focused somewhere in the middle of his chest, avoiding his gaze.

"I'll call you tomorrow about getting started, J—" her voice seemed to fail for a moment "—ack. Jack. Tomorrow. Bye!"

The door slammed shut after her.

Finally able to move, Jack flew to the outside door and wrenched it open. Kitty was rounding the corner of the building, out of sight.

"What the hell just happened?" Oz asked from behind him.

Jack leaned against the doorframe. That was a very good question. He felt as if he'd just cycled fifty miles. Uphill. With an erection.

"Two things, Oz. The first one is that I just met the woman from my dream." He rubbed sweat from his face, and then adjusted his jeans. "And the second one is that I've proven once and for all that I can get a hard-on."

Oz clapped him on the shoulder. "Kitty is your dream woman? Excellent."

"Yeah. Excellent."

Oz narrowed his eyes. "Somehow, Jack, you don't sound as enthusiastic as you should be."

"There's a problem. I broke her heart ten years ago. Remember?"

"I am a professional. I am a professional. I am—ouch!"

Kitty winced as her ankle twisted on the gravel of the parking lot. She staggered the last few steps to her Mercedes and leaned against its polished silver surface. In the window, the reflection of her face was deathly pale and wide-eyed.

She'd been doing so well. She'd convinced herself she could deal with whatever her crazy fate threw at her. When she'd walked into the Delphi and only seen the tall, shaggy-haired blond hunk with the big hands and the huge smile, she'd breathed a sigh of relief. Jack was dark-haired and lithe, not blond and gigantic.

Then he'd told her his name. And Kitty's stomach had tried to crawl up her throat and down her legs simultaneously.

Oscar Strummer had been *his* best friend in high school.

It was then that the alarm bells had starting ringing loud and clear. *Stay calm*, she'd reminded herself. *Stay focused. Remember how much you have at stake here. You are an adult, and what happened in high school doesn't matter anymore.*

Wrong. Jack's voice had nearly destroyed her. It had felt as if her body had shut itself down; it had been as much effort as she'd been able to summon to turn around and look at him. And then even more effort, once she'd seen him, not to fall into a puddle at his feet.

He looked good. Even covered with dirt, in shabby clothes, with a big black smudge on his forehead, he looked incredible. The beautiful boy she remembered from school had turned into a devastatingly gorgeous man.

He had the same brown eyes, the same black hair pushed back from his forehead, the same freshness to his skin, but his face was stronger now and his chin was shadowed with black stubble. His body had filled out; he was still lean, but now he was muscular, too. He was taller. He had dark hair on his forearms and just peeking over the collar of his T-shirt. He didn't wear his high school ring anymore. But what hadn't changed in the slightest from the last time Kitty had seen Jack, ten years ago, was his energy.

He moved quickly, fluidly. Words tripped off his tongue. His mouth and his eyes were in constant expressive motion. It was just as mesmerizing as she remembered. More. When he'd held out his hand for her to shake he'd raised one eyebrow in an impossibly endearing expression that had made him look both boyish and sexy.

But she'd survived it. She'd kept her cool. In fact, she'd kept her cool so amazingly well that, in some corner of her brain, Kitty Giroux Clifford had been looking at herself with serious respect. When he'd offered her the job, Kitty had known she'd won.

And then she'd had to go look him in the eyes and blow the whole thing.

"Oh, God, God, God." Kitty slapped the hardtop of her convertible. "What have I gotten myself into?"

From the minute she'd met his eyes, Kitty had felt as if she were paralyzed. It was exactly the same as it had been in high school. One look from those brown eyes and she melted, she froze, she felt about a million things all at once and she couldn't decide on any of them. Her heart stopped beating. She stopped breathing. Her tongue became a lump in her mouth, incapable of saying anything except for the one syllable that was the most important word for her in the entire universe at that moment.

Jack.

She'd felt fourteen again. Pinned by those eyes as she had been in the corridor of her high school when he'd deigned to look at her. Weak-kneed, butterfly-stomached, sweaty-handed.

He'd taken all of her professionalism, all of her control, and zapped it out of existence.

Kitty groaned. "Why can't he be fat? Or bald?" She kicked a rock with her ivory shoe and paced up and down the parking lot. "Why can't he have lots of zits or something now?"

But no. He was gorgeous. And more than that, there was something else she couldn't forget, something that was making her knees still tremble—what had passed between her and Jack Taylor not ten minutes ago had been a lot more than a look exchanged across a high-school corridor. Because they had both grown into adults, and the signals that had been zinging between them were very adult signals indeed.

Pure sex.

Heedless of her light-colored clothing, Kitty leaned back against a battered yellow Beetle as a wave of heat swept through her again. The minute Jack had met her eyes she'd felt more than attraction. More than lust, even.

She'd felt as if she and Jack had been actually having sex right there in the lobby of that broken-down, beautiful cinema.

She'd been able to feel his hands on her body, stroking her

to heights of pleasure she'd never imagined before. She'd felt his hot, wet mouth on hers, and all over her skin. Good God, she'd felt him inside her, surging, full of energy and life and passion.

She could still feel it now. Kitty closed her eyes and tilted her head back. It was melting, and powerful, and joyous, and exciting, and oh, so arousing. Her clothes rubbed against her in ways she'd never noticed before. Her body was one huge erogenous zone just waiting to be satisfied.

Kitty ran her hand down the heated skin of her neck and thought about what it would be like if Jack touched her that way. What she would have done if he had stepped closer and kissed her.

Of course, she'd had to escape. Kitty might have bad luck, but she wasn't stupid. There was no way she was going to turn into a puddle in front of Jack Taylor. The boy who had shattered her dreams in high school. The man who could help or crush her career with a single rise of one eyebrow.

The man who represented everything, absolutely everything she feared.

Kitty's eyes flew open. All the sensuality that had overcome her turned instantly into clammy, heart-seizing embarrassment.

She'd said "wicked excited". She'd said "totally awesome".

She'd sounded exactly like a sixteen-year-old, wanna-be cheerleader.

"I am a total airhead," she said to the parking lot.

Well. There was no alternative. She couldn't give up this job. It was just what she needed. And she obviously wasn't going to be able to avoid Jack, either. So what she had to do was to summon all her reserves of professionalism and not let Jack Taylor turn her into a helpless, throbbing bundle of hormones.

"I will not let Jack Taylor turn me into a helpless, throbbing bundle of hormones," she told the parking lot. "I am a grown woman of twenty-seven. I don't let boys affect me this way anymore."

Kitty straightened and tucked a few wayward strands of hair behind her ears. She took a deep breath.

And then she ducked behind the Beetle, because Jack Taylor had just rounded the corner in front of her.

He'd been running, and he did that with the same natural agility that he did everything. He was so damn gorgeous. So perfect in everything except personality. And here she was, crouched beside a car in high heels and an expensive suit, hoping like hell he hadn't seen her.

Kitty risked a look, peeking up over the Beetle's backside. Jack stood on the sidewalk in front of the parking lot, looking intently down the street and pushing his hair back from his forehead with one hand. Kitty stooped back behind the car.

"This is ridiculous," she muttered. "I've got to get out of here." She edged toward the front of the car, shuffling her shoes along the gravel in tiny, high-heeled steps. She could go round between the wall and the Beetle's front bumper, and get to the door of her Mercedes without being seen.

She reached the wall and considered the gap between it and the bumper. She could just about squeeze through, but her suit would suffer. Kitty looked at the wall, and she looked at her suit. It had cost her a lot of money—money she no longer had for a replacement. She could ruin her suit. Or she could let Jack see her.

Hopeful, she peered up above the Beetle's hood and was rewarded with the sight of Jack running down the street away from her. She jumped up, hurried to her car, hurled herself inside and left two trails of rubber on the gravel behind her as she reversed out of the parking lot. She turned the car in the opposite direction to the way Jack had run. It wasn't the way home, but she decided she'd rather take the long route than pass Jack.

It took at least four blocks before Kitty could slow down. She stopped at a red light and looked down at herself. She'd put a hole in her nylons when she'd knelt down, her skirt was smeared with dust, and one of her shoes had a long brown scuff on it.

This really was ridiculous. She felt a smile creep across her face.

"Wrong, Kitty. You're not grown up yet. And you still don't know how to deal with boys."

CHAPTER THREE

"'AMBITION: To own my own cinema, and make my life like a movie.'"

Kitty read aloud from the yearbook opened on her lap. Jack's senior picture grinned from the page, a photo of a boy confident that he could conquer the world.

He hadn't signed her yearbook, of course. But Kitty's best friend Marie had drawn a heart around Jack's picture, and had added another ambition below his own: "To marry Kitty Giroux and live happily ever after."

Kitty snorted. At least his cinema ambition was going to come true. She flipped forward in the book to find her own picture in the junior class. There she was, arm in arm with Marie, smiling with her mouth closed to hide her braces. Her hair frizzed around her skinny shoulders and, though the photograph was black and white, some joker had made up for it by drawing a big arrow pointing to Kitty's head and writing "CARROTS!" in magic marker next to it.

She ran a finger tenderly over the picture. The girl in that photograph did not look as though she was confident of conquering the world. She looked a lot more as though the world was going to conquer her. And as though she was afraid that it already had.

Kitty leaned across her narrow, pink-quilted bed and plucked another yearbook from the shelf. Her senior picture in this one was in color. She'd had the braces off, she had makeup on and she'd spent an hour and a half with hair straighteners before going to the photographer's studio. Her smile showed all of her perfect, braceless teeth and her eyes shone. Her chin was tilted up. Her ambition was simply: "To be the best."

A person who hadn't known Kitty her last year in high school would have said that this photograph showed a happy girl who was determined that her future was going to be bright. Kitty knew what the photograph really showed. The smile, the eyes, the hair, the chin, the makeup, they were all meant to convey a single message: *I am going to succeed. Despite my red hair, my freckles, and my secondhand clothes. Despite the fact that I haven't seen my father since I was thirteen and he walked out on us. Despite the fact that Jack Taylor dumped me for another girl on prom night.*

She'd wanted nothing more than to finally grow up and get control of her own life.

And it hadn't worked. Three minutes in a room with Jack Taylor, and she was right back to being that frizzy-haired, insecure girl again.

Kitty sighed and stretched back on her bed. This trip down memory lane wasn't doing her any good. She had moved on since she'd graduated high school, but she'd never know it from the way she'd been thinking for the past few hours.

Being in the bedroom she'd grown up in didn't help. It was like a time warp back ten years, down to the stuffed animals on the bed and the Madonna posters on the wall. She really had to get her own place. Soon.

"Kitty!" Her mother called from downstairs. "You have a visitor!"

Good. Probably her cousin Paula with the kids. Exactly the sort of break Kitty needed. She jumped off the bed and went hurtling down the stairs two at a time, sure-footed from years of practice. She cleared the last three with a single leap and landed with a slide of her sock-clad feet on the kitchen linoleum.

"Hey! Careful." Hands closed on her arms, and she found herself face-to-face with Jack Taylor. "I like women throwing themselves at me, but not literally."

"Jack!" Kitty stepped back, feeling the blood rush to her cheeks. And to other places. "What are you doing here?" She rubbed her arms where he'd touched her bare skin.

"Oz said you'd told him your mother still lived in town. So I drove over to ask where you were living, and your mother said you happened to be here."

"Jack tells me he's the owner of the Delphi, Kitty. Isn't that a coincidence, you two meeting up again after all these years?"

Kitty shot her mother a look. "But what are you doing here?" she asked Jack, again.

He didn't seem to notice her rudeness. "We didn't get the chance to discuss our ideas for the Delphi in any detail this afternoon, so I thought I'd take you out to dinner and we could talk about it."

He'd showered since this afternoon, and shaved and changed his clothes to clean khakis and a white cotton button-down shirt. His tanned skin and his dark hair made the white shirt look bright in the fluorescent lights of the kitchen.

He looked wonderful. Compared with his high-school picture, he looked about a thousand times better. He had not only confidence, but a masculine presence that made the kitchen seem a whole lot smaller.

And he was here. In her mother's kitchen. Far, far too close to home for Kitty's comfort.

"I'm busy tonight, thanks. I'm visiting with my mother." No way was she going to tell him that she was living here, not visiting. "Why don't I come to the Delphi tomorrow morning and we'll discuss it then?"

"I was going to start dinner in a minute," her mother piped up. "It's no trouble to cook for one more, Jack, and then you can stay for dinner here and talk about your theater with Kitty."

Jack smiled. "Thank you, Mrs. Giroux, that's very kind. I'd love to stay for dinner."

No. *No!* Kitty had an instant vision of the three of them sitting around the kitchen table, her mother warming to Jack's charming smile. Chatting away while she served the chicken casserole and green beans. Telling him about how nice it was to have Kitty living back at home, and that Kitty was running her business out of the spare room now, but with this new contract at the Delphi she'd be able to get an office of her own again, and wasn't it strange that they knew each other from high school, and, Kitty, didn't you go to the prom with Jack Taylor? While Jack's smile got wider and wider, and Kitty slowly collapsed into a small heap of pure humiliation.

"No, Mom, thanks, but Jack and I have a lot to discuss, and you'd just get bored. Can't it wait till tomorrow?"

She turned to Jack, but he shook his head, that smile still there. "No, I'm eager to discuss it thoroughly with you tonight."

The way he said "thoroughly" made it sound to her oversensitive ears as if he were talking about doing something else thoroughly with her. Something a lot more hands-on than discussion.

Katherine Giroux Clifford, get a grip. Your high-school crush has turned into a case of terminal lust, but you are working for this man. And he's not to be trusted.

"So, can I take you out to dinner, or will we be enjoying your mother's home cooking?"

She didn't have to think twice. Going out with Jack Taylor was an incredibly bad idea, but staying home and risking her mother's chattiness was an even worse one. Let alone risking him getting past the kitchen and seeing the rest of the house, and how shabby it was. "I'll put on my shoes."

Her mother followed her into the front room. "He's very handsome, isn't he? Is this a date?"

Kitty shoved on her shoes and picked up her bag. "No, Mom, this isn't a date. He wants to discuss the theater. I won't be late."

"Oh, be as late as you want. You haven't been on any dates since you got to Portland. You deserve some fun."

She closed her eyes for a moment, took a deep breath for courage and kissed her mother on the cheek. "Goodbye, Mom." She walked past Jack in the kitchen and opened the back door. "Let's go."

Outside, her convertible was parked next to her mother's battered Japanese hatchback. "Nice car," Jack commented. "Is it yours?"

"The Mercedes is." For now. She ran her eyes over its stylish lines, and remembered driving into Portland in it, six months ago. How optimistic she'd felt—the fatherless, shabby kid coming back home in an expensive car and designer clothes.

Jack led her to his car, a red four-wheel drive. Kitty wasn't surprised to see that it was the latest model. His family had always been well-off; his father was an architect and they lived in a gorgeous house on Peak's Island. In Jack's world, a new car was nothing special.

"Do you like seafood?" he asked her as he opened the passenger door for her.

"I'm from Maine. What do you think?" She buckled her seat belt and looked straight out the windshield.

"Great." He got in his own side and started up the car. "It really is good to see you again, Kitty."

Liar. She didn't know what he was up to, but she had a pretty good idea, and it wasn't a high-school reunion.

"I like to be called Katherine now."

"Grown out of the nickname, huh?" He looked over at her. "You've definitely grown up."

His voice and his eyes on her started that wave of heat again. Kitty crossed her arms over her chest to hide her nipples, which had thrilled to attention. She pressed her thighs together. "It's been ten years. It would be surprising if I hadn't."

"Yes, but you've done a particularly good job at it. So what have you been doing with yourself the past ten years, Katherine, besides growing up so spectacularly well?"

"I've been working for an interior design firm in Los Angeles. I only recently moved back to Maine to set up my own business."

"Really?" he said. "LA is a wonderful place. I lived there when I was a kid, before my parents moved us to Maine."

I know you did, Kitty thought. She watched the road in front of them.

She also knew that one of the reasons she'd moved to LA herself was because Jack came from there, although that fact was so incredibly pathetic that she shoved it aside as fast as she could. But not fast enough to stop herself from wondering how many more of her life-changing decisions, whether she'd known it or not, had been influenced by Jack Taylor.

Her marriage, for example. And her divorce.

Because Sam had been like Jack, only safer, hadn't he? Charming, rich, handsome; he'd even been involved in the movie industry, as a lawyer. The only difference was how she'd felt when she'd been around him. She'd never, for example, had to press her thighs together in Sam's presence. When she'd been with Sam she'd never felt dizzy, excited, about to fall down a delicious, dangerous precipice. Not as she felt now, with Jack.

She'd never felt this way with anyone except for Jack.

But safe Sam had left her anyway, for another woman. She hadn't been good enough for him, in the end. Just as she hadn't been good enough for Jack. Or good enough to keep her father from leaving.

"So should I also call you Mrs. Clifford?" His smile, even

in the shadowy light of the car, even when she couldn't see it because she was looking everywhere but at him, was dazzling.

She'd been right. He was flirting with her.

Not surprising. As Jack had said, she'd grown up. She knew she was reasonably good-looking now. She was used to men flirting with her. Why would Jack Taylor, a flirtaholic if ever there was one, be any exception?

And then there was that moment that had passed between them this afternoon. For Kitty, who'd had a world-class crush on Jack Taylor since she was fourteen, the attraction wasn't a surprise. But the power of it was. Surely he'd noticed at least some of how intensely she'd responded to him. He probably thought she'd be an easy conquest.

"Go on, put me out of my misery," he said. "Are you married?"

"I'm divorced."

She could hear him letting out a breath. "Good. I mean, not good, because divorce is a very sad thing. But good for me, because I really didn't want you to be married."

She almost laughed. He sounded flustered and genuinely relieved. Of course it was an act, all part of the Jack Taylor charm, but it was—well, charming.

Kitty tightened her arms around her chest. *That's the danger*, she reminded herself. *He's all charm and no heart.*

"Jack, I don't see what my marital status has to do with my job. I came out with you to discuss renovating the Delphi, and that's all. I wish you'd stop flirting with me."

The pause was so long that she risked turning so she could see Jack's face fully for the first time since she'd met his eyes in the cinema. He was staring at the road, his eyebrows drawn down. It looked as if he was biting the inside of his lip.

"I'm sorry I made you uncomfortable, Katherine."

And that was the second time in less than five minutes that Jack had sounded sincere.

"I know we weren't really friends after the prom, back in

high school," Jack continued. "But I hope we can put that behind us."

"My thoughts exactly," Kitty replied.

"It was sort of a shock seeing you."

"Tell me about it."

"But there's been a lot of water under the bridge now, Katherine. We're not teenagers anymore, and I like to think I've developed a little bit of sensitivity and tact."

It wasn't an apology. But she'd never wanted an apology out of Jack Taylor, anyway. She'd wanted him to love her, and she was never going to get that, and she might as well grow up and deal with it.

"You're right," she said. "It's been a long time, and we're not teenagers anymore."

"Tell me to shut up if you want me to, but I'm sorry you had to go through a divorce. I hope it wasn't a bad one."

"It was perfectly amicable," Kitty said. "Sam is a very nice man, and we're still friends."

"I guess if you have to get a divorce, that's the best kind to get."

And it had been a surprisingly easy one. When Sam had gone back to his first wife, her heart hadn't been broken. Kitty supposed she'd had enough of that in high school to last a lifetime. Maybe she didn't have anything left to break.

What had hurt was the failure. She'd refused alimony, even though Sam had insisted. Mostly because she wanted independence, but partly because she knew the monthly payments would just remind her of how she hadn't been able to make even a safe relationship work.

"You've never been married yourself?" Kitty knew the answer before she asked the question.

"Never been tempted," Jack said. "I've been too busy having fun."

"I'll bet."

She glanced at Jack again. His profile was stunningly gorgeous, as always. Straight nose, strong jaw. He still looked as if he were thinking hard about something. For a man who'd just said he'd been busy having fun, he looked very serious.

For the first time she found herself considering whether Jack Taylor had grown up in more ways than physically since that horrible prom night. If maybe they were both completely different people.

He shook his head slightly, as if he were clearing it, and flashed another one of those thigh-melting smiles at her.

"I'm excited to be working with you, Katherine," Jack said. "The Delphi is incredibly important to me. I've wanted to own it since I was a kid. This is my big chance."

"I've always loved the building," Kitty agreed.

"It's amazing." He shot her another smile, this one friendly. "You never used to be a film buff in high school."

"No, I'm more a real-life kind of person. I'm attracted to the Delphi itself, not the movies. It's a striking example of art deco design."

"Have you seen *Casablanca* yet?"

She actually felt herself smiling. "No, I haven't. I told you that ten years ago, Jack. I don't believe you remember it."

"How could I forget that you haven't seen *Casablanca*? It's unnatural. Have you seen *Gone With the Wind*?"

"No."

"American Beauty? Apocalypse Now? Forrest Gump?"

"No."

He glanced over at her. "Are you sure you're alive and living in the twenty-first century?"

"They're just movies, Jack."

Jack made an outraged sound. "Someday, Ms. Clifford, you'll recognize the absolute heresy of that statement."

They pulled up in front of the restaurant. Jack reached into the back seat and pulled out a large folder. "I've got photographs in here and some notes I've made with my ideas for the

Delphi. I've even done a few sketches, though, since my drawing skills are worse than a four-year-old's, you'll probably laugh at them."

He looked across at her, smiling, and Kitty smiled back. Her heart fluttered in her chest, but somehow this time it wasn't as scary.

Jack held the door of the restaurant open for her. It looked pretty fancy: linen tablecloths, a huge flower arrangement near the entrance. "Am I dressed for this place?" Kitty asked, conscious of her jeans and short-sleeved top. If she'd known she was going to a business dinner in a nice restaurant, she'd have dressed to impress. She had an image to uphold, after all.

"You're perfect."

Kitty wasn't sure if that was flirting or not, but before she had time to question it a pretty blond woman approached them. "Hi, Jack!" she beamed.

"Hi, Anna. Table for two?"

The blonde led them across the room to a table in the corner. They looked at the menus, they gave the waiter their orders, they took sips of the white wine Jack had selected. Then Jack pushed the glasses and flowers to the side of the table and spread out his folder.

"The Delphi is more than a building to me," he began, and Kitty saw that light come into his face again. She pulled her chair forward.

"It's a...a temple of visions," he said. "It's a place where anything can happen. Where any wish you ever had can come true, even if it's only for a little while."

This was it. Emotion in his voice. Kitty knew from professional experience that when a client started giving you their emotional impressions, you should listen carefully. It was the key to going beyond color schemes and fabric swatches, to what they really wanted out of the design.

"Is that what you love about the movies?" she asked. Ignoring the fact that her interest was beyond professional. That her heart had skipped in her chest at hearing Jack sound so passionate.

"Yeah. The possibilities, the dreams made real. It's always been something magical for me. Whatever's happening in your life, when you're at the movies, everything is okay. The worst thing that can happen to you is that you don't like the film. It's a total escape from real life."

"You want the Delphi to be a dream come true," she said. "A place that's beyond the boundaries of real life, where people can forget themselves."

Jack nodded vigorously. "Exactly. That's it. Look."

He pulled out a sheaf of photographs and pointed out the features he wanted to keep and what he wanted to change, showing her his notes. He'd thought about everything from the lighting to the popcorn maker. All the time speaking with that energy, that vitality that was pure Jack.

Their meals arrived, and though Kitty took a bite of her grilled fish, she didn't taste it. She was too excited. Half of her mind was on Jack, and the other was on what he was describing. She pictured the vast, elegant space of the cinema.

"The ceiling will need to be replastered and rewired," she mused, "but we'll photograph the stars so we can reproduce them exactly. We have to keep the stars, because—"

"It's part of the illusion. Yes. What do we use for that—silver paint, or—?"

"Silver foil. Real silver. Even at that height, it'll look richer than paint. That's probably what's up there already."

"Excellent. Excellent." He ran his hand through his hair, leaving it in disarray. "Now, what about the—?" He gestured in the air with his hands, forming an arch shape.

"Proscenium arch?"

He snapped his fingers. "That's it. What do you think we should do with that?"

Kitty impatiently shoved aside her plate and scootched her

chair around to his side of the table. She pulled a pencil out of her bag and copied one of his photographs on the back of one of his sheets of notes.

"Here's what it's like now," she said, drawing rapidly. "It looks like we're missing a top piece."

"I was told it fell down in the eighties and they replaced it with that scrolling. I don't know what the original was like."

"Right. But I imagine this leaf motif here carried through. What we can do is make more of these stylized leaves, and hide lights inside them to illuminate the ceiling." She added her ideas to the sketch as she spoke. "The whole thing gives the feeling of a temple, only an art deco interpretation."

Jack lifted his eyes from her sketch to her face, and Kitty suddenly realized how close they were sitting.

Their shoulders nearly touched; his hand rested on the paper she'd been drawing on. His fingers were so close to hers that she could feel the warmth from them.

"You see it," he said. "You see what I want."

Her eyes focused on his mouth: his lower lip was full and generous; his top lip dipped down in the middle teasingly. She could hear the rustle of his cotton shirt.

He raised his hand and cupped her chin, his long fingers against her cheek. He tilted her head upwards so her eyes met his. "Do you see me?"

Did she see him? She couldn't see anything else. His eyes were dark, warm, deep. They seemed to see right inside her. And for the second time today the small distance between them seemed to dissolve away and they seemed to be joined more intimately than she'd ever felt.

She yanked in a breath and, though the cooler air refreshed her burning body, the air was full of Jack. His woody cologne, the wine on his lips, the smell of his clean white shirt, a warm smell that she knew was the scent of his skin.

In her confused mind it all became wrapped up in the rich

brown of his eyes. When they moved, reading her gaze, she felt as if his body had moved and pulled her closer. Their pupils expanded and she opened her mouth, ready for the parted lips of his kiss. And when they dipped down for a split second, she felt as if the palm of his hand were scorching down her body, tracing a path of fire over her breasts and straight between her legs, melting everything it touched.

His thumb touched her open mouth, and Kitty, entranced, let her tongue slip forward to taste his skin. Salt. Warmth. Ridged thumbprint, as uniquely his as his eyes still on her. Jack made a sound deep in his throat and it reverberated within her own chest. The tip of his thumb slid between her lips, into her mouth.

Oh, God, this was Jack, inside her, filling her senses with just that small piece of flesh. She closed her lips around him, closed her eyes and felt only the pleasure of his touch there, between her teeth like the most luscious fruit she'd ever tasted.

"Kitty," Jack said, and his voice was rough, nearly choking, "I've felt this way since seeing you again. It's—I just can't quite believe it's you."

She felt his other hand touching the hair beside her face, stroking a strand of it, touching, briefly, her ear. She opened her eyes and saw his gaze still intent on her face.

The intensity was too much; she felt as if she'd drunk a bottle of wine instead of half a glass. Her head spun, her body throbbed, and she wasn't quite sure what to think.

Kitty drew her head back from Jack's hand, releasing his thumb, and stood. "Excuse me a second, I need the ladies'."

Her voice sounded unreal to her. Dizzy, wobbly-legged, her mouth still full of the taste of Jack, Kitty made her way across the dining room and down the narrow staircase.

She leaned against the wall outside the door of the ladies' room and attempted to make her breathing normal. Could she make sense of this?

Could she explain to herself why she had just taken a man's thumb into her mouth and felt as if she'd had full intercourse with him, less than an hour into their first date, which wasn't even a date, and after she'd told him in no uncertain terms that she didn't want him to flirt with her?

Of course she could. There was one simple explanation: she wanted Jack Taylor, with a sharp longing that made her teen-age crush seem like a silly toy.

No. No. This was a very, very bad idea. Jack Taylor was a flirt. Jack Taylor was a player. He always had been.

But he's changed, said a little voice in her head. *He's not just a flirt. There's passion underneath that charm. He really cares about the Delphi, which means he can really care about something.*

"The last thing I need right now is another man who's not right for me." Her words echoed sharply in the small corridor, and drowned out that little voice.

But not quite.

Kitty shook her head, took a deep breath and went back up-stairs to where Jack waited for her.

He stood when she returned. She pulled her chair back to her side of the table, but he caught her hand in his as she sat down. His skin felt nearly hot enough to burn her.

"Kitty," he said, "let's get out of here. Come home with me."

He ran his thumb, the one she'd tasted, over the back of her hand. She grasped her water glass with her other hand and drank from it. The water didn't give her any answers.

"Why?" she asked with a mouth that was, impossibly, dry.

Jack smiled. His left eyebrow quirked up. "I think that's obvious, isn't it?"

Yes. The desire between them was about as subtle as a bull-dozer. Kitty swallowed again, and knew that she'd never wanted anything so much in her life as she wanted to go home with Jack Taylor tonight.

Except, maybe, ten years ago, when she'd wanted Jack Taylor to take her to the prom.

"Hi, Jack!"

A woman's voice startled her enough so she could tear her eyes away from Jack's. A brunette dressed in the black skirt and white shirt of a waitress stood beside them.

"Hi, Brigid," said Jack, and then he turned his attention back to Kitty as the waitress walked away.

But that small interruption had been enough. A puzzle piece clicked inside Kitty's head.

"Did you date that woman?" she asked. "And the hostess, too? Is that how you know them?"

He shrugged and nodded. "Yeah. Not anymore, though."

"And did you take them both home with you, Jack?"

His eyebrows drew together. She saw him bite his inner lip. She waited.

"Does that matter?" he asked.

She pulled her hand away. "Did you sleep with them?"

His frown got deeper. He looked down at the tablecloth, and then back into her face, and down again. Finally he met her eyes again.

"Not together," he said.

Kitty stood up. "Jack, I'd like to leave now."

He stood, too. "Kitty, I'm sorr—"

She didn't wait for him. She walked straight through the door and into the cool evening.

It didn't cool her down. Jack's car was parked by the restaurant, but she paced up and down the sidewalk. She could picture what he was doing while she stomped. He had to put all his pictures and notes back in the folder. He had to pay for the meal, and say a fond goodbye to the beautiful Brigid. Then he had to stop and talk to Anna on the way out, smiling and flirting like crazy. Maybe making a date for tomorrow night. And then he could come outside to her, finally, and touch her elbow as she kept on walking. Which he did.

"I'm sorry about that," he said.

"Sure. It was nice to meet your girlfriends." She didn't stop walking.

He kept pace with her. "Kitty. Katherine. It's over with Brigid and Anna. It's been over for a long time."

"A long time. Is that days, or hours?" She stopped and glared at him full in the face. "Did you actually take me to that restaurant in some twisted scheme to play your women off each other? Because I'm not impressed, Jack. Not at all."

"No. Honestly." He took her shoulders in his hands and held her there, looking down into her face. "I didn't think."

"Hi, Jack."

The voice rang out across the sidewalk, and Kitty saw an auburn-haired woman walking toward them on the arm of a big, football-player type man. The woman flashed a smile, and Kitty saw the man look from Jack to the redhead and back again, an unmistakable frown of jealousy forming between his close-set eyes.

"Hi, Treena," Jack answered.

"Another one of your girlfriends, Jack?" Kitty said through gritted teeth.

Jack dropped his hands from Kitty's shoulders. Answer enough.

That was it.

"Take me home," she said. Jack followed her to the car.

One might be a coincidence. Two might be bad luck. But running into three of Jack's girlfriends in a single night was an unmistakable message from whatever poor excuse for a guardian angel was looking after her.

CHAPTER FOUR

Now this *is sexual frustration*, Jack thought as he neared the Delphi.

He hadn't had any sleep after his date with Kitty, though he'd tried. He'd lain down in bed, hoping to have the dream again. No luck. He remembered an article he'd read years ago in a magazine about being able to control the content of your dreams. Something about your subconscious; Oz would understand it. You had to relax and gently steer your thoughts toward what you wanted to dream about.

He'd failed. Relaxing and thinking about Kitty were mutually exclusive. Every time he thought about her, his body turned into a bundle of aching, hungry need. There were so many things he wanted to do with her.

The night had been spent turning in his bed, envisioning unbuttoning her blouse, peeling her jeans off those long legs, abandoning himself to the feeling of her skin.

And every single one of those visions ended with her words dashing over him like a cold bucket of water: "I'm not impressed, Jack. Not at all."

So this afternoon he felt hyper-aware, hyper-aroused and hyper-grumpy. Every step from his house to the Delphi made his head feel heavier, made his muscles more tense. He approached the Delphi's heavy front door and saw that it was slightly ajar. He pushed it open and went inside the building. Oz stood in the lobby, holding his toolbox and looking mighty pleased with himself.

"Why are you looking so happy?" Jack snapped.

Oz didn't seem to notice his sharp tone. "I covered up the trapdoor so you won't fall through it again," he said. "And I've been waiting here to find out how it went last night with your dream woman."

"My dream woman hates me."

"Not surprising. Love and hate are, at their base, the same emotion."

"Who said anything about love? I just need her to stop hating me long enough to sleep with me."

Oz stroked the blond bristle on his chin thoughtfully. "How long have your parents been happily married, Jack?"

"Thirty years last month. We had a big party. You were there, remember?"

"Don't you want what they have?"

"Yes. No. Maybe." Jack shook his head to clear it. "I'm so horny I can't think straight. You should have seen Kitty in my car last night when I was taking her back to her mother's. If she'd had a knife, I'd be walking funny today." He kicked the nearest wall. "I feel like I'm walking funny as it is."

"What happened?"

"We ran into Anna."

"Ah."

"And Brigid. And Treena."

"Finally, you are discovering the wages of sin." Oz rubbed his hands together. "I'm going to enjoy watching this one."

"It's not funny, Oz."

"Come on. You knew this wasn't going to be easy. You dumped this woman for another girl on prom night. That's got to hurt."

"That was a long time ago. And I didn't kiss Melissa

Beauchamp, Melissa Beauchamp kissed *me*. And besides, you weren't even at the prom, you were at some math weekend for geniuses or something."

"I remember it being all over the school on Monday, though," Oz said. "I wasn't in school for five minutes before I'd heard from three different people that my best friend had taken Kitty Giroux to the prom and then kissed another girl on the dance floor in front of her. Remember I told you off for being irresponsible?"

Jack rolled his eyes. "How could I forget?"

"Face it, Jack. Your past has come back to haunt you, and she's gorgeous."

"Shut up, Oz."

"That's what you said after prom night, too. You always tell me to shut up when you know I'm right."

He loved Oz; they'd been best friends since they were kids. But sometimes it felt as if they were slotting into preordained roles. Jack the popular one. Oz the brainy one. Jack the fun-loving, carefree one. Oz the responsible, thoughtful one.

And Oz was right, usually. But every now and then Jack wished Oz would stop being his conscience and let him figure out his conscience for himself.

What was wrong with wanting to feel good instead of feeling bad, anyway? Wanting to have fun instead of getting cooped up with obligations?

Okay, so he'd been irresponsible in the past. He'd avoided commitment with women. But that didn't mean he was a jerk or anything. It didn't mean he couldn't commit, if he wanted to, someday.

He could. If he wanted. He was a nice guy.

Kitty doesn't think you're a nice guy, a voice in his head told him. He pushed it aside.

"You're not right, Oz," he said. "It was a long time ago, and sure, I shouldn't have done that to Kitty. I didn't mean for it to get all over the school. And I did try to apologize to her. But it wasn't a big deal. I mean, look at Kitty—she's obviously successful, she drives this really expensive car and she's beautiful. It obviously hasn't ruined her life or anything."

Oz folded his arms and shook his head. "I am perpetually astounded at your capacity for denial, Jack."

"Hi. Am I interrupting?"

Her voice.

Jack stood stock-still. When, in the heated, futile hours of the night before, had he begun to miss her voice?

"Hi, Kitty." Oz, apparently unburdened by paralyzing desire, approached her where she stood just inside the open inner door of the cinema. She wore a slim light brown skirt that emphasized the lines of her waist and hips, and a fitted matching jacket. Tailored, impeccable and luscious.

"Hi, Oz. Hello, Jack."

He knew exactly when he'd started to miss her voice. The minute he'd dropped her off at her mother's house. And it had grown with the hours they'd been apart, until now, when she said his name and he nearly groaned with pleasure.

"Hi, Katherine," he managed, and joined her and Oz near the door. When he got closer he could see she was wearing lipstick, a deep rose color that made her mouth look even more impossibly lush. *I've touched her lips,* he thought, and his skin heated up a few more degrees.

"Bye, Oz," he said.

"What? Oh yeah." Oz picked up his toolbox. "I think I've got some hammering to do somewhere. See you later, Kitty."

Kitty smiled at him as he left the lobby, then turned to Jack, her smile gone.

"I came here to sort something out. I'm very interested in the Delphi, and I want to work on it with you. I wouldn't want our professional relationship to be affected by our disagreement—" her businesslike tone faltered on the last word, but it was back again in an instant "—last night. So I've brought you some sketches I've done based on the ideas you were telling me about."

She held out a plastic portfolio, and Jack took it automatically. "Thanks."

"I think we can work well together if we can keep things from being personal. I understand if you feel differently. But I'd like you to have a look at my sketches before you decide to consider another designer."

Consider another designer? When all he could think about was being with Kitty? In bed, up against a wall, on his kitchen table, on the stage in front of the movie screen?

"Um. Thanks. I will."

"Good. I'll talk to you after you've had a chance to look those over, then. Bye." And then she was gone, leaving behind only the whiff of her vanilla perfume, her portfolio of drawings and a fierce hunger in Jack.

Sexual frustration was turning his brains to mush. That had to be the explanation for why Jack was standing on the sidewalk outside the Delphi the next day, dialing Kitty's number into his cell phone. For the fourth time this afternoon.

She didn't answer it. She never answered it. Instead, her service picked up. "Hello. Ms. Clifford can't take your call right now, would you like to leave a message?"

"Hi, Linda, it's Jack Taylor again."

"Hi, Jack." Linda's voice instantly became cozy.

"I was wondering, do you think Ms. Clifford will pick up her messages any time soon?"

"I can't read her mind. She usually calls in the afternoons. So tell me, Jack, are you as sexy as your voice sounds?"

Sex-starved, maybe. More so in the past three days than he'd been in the previous eleven celibate months. "Couldn't say, Linda. Could you read me back the messages I've left already?"

She chuckled. "You asked her to call you at eleven this morning. At one-thirty you checked to see if she'd picked up the message yet. At two-fifteen you said you were going to the theater and she could reach you on your cell phone. At two twenty-five you called to leave your cell phone number in case she didn't have it. It's now three forty-seven. I think this woman is playing hard to get with you, Jack."

"Okay, I'll leave one more message. Could you tell her I have some important things to discuss with her about the Delphi, and she should come here as soon as possible?"

"Sure thing, Jack. Listen, if she doesn't turn up, I get off work at seven, and I always go to Gritty's for a beer after work. Like to meet me?"

"Very tempting, but I don't think so, Linda."

He stopped himself, and looked at the phone in his hand for a moment. Why was he flirting with Linda? He wasn't interested in Linda.

Force of habit, he guessed. A habit he should be breaking.

"You know where to find me," Linda was saying when he put the phone back to his ear. "Bye for now."

He turned the phone off and leaned back against the brick wall. Kitty was avoiding him. She had to be. There was no other explanation for why she had her phone turned off, why she didn't collect her messages.

But what else could he do? He couldn't change the past, but he was convinced he could persuade Kitty not to hate him, if she gave him a chance. His charm wasn't rusty; Linda proved that. He still looked the same; Anna, Brigid, and Treena's jealous boyfriend proved that. And she was attracted to him; the intense, wonderful moments in the restaurant proved that.

Did they ever prove that. They'd also proven some other important facts: that Jack Taylor couldn't close his eyes without the image of Kitty's smouldering gaze rising before his vision.

That Jack Taylor was obsessed with this woman as he'd never been in all the twenty-eight years of his life.

And that Jack Taylor had absolutely no idea what to do about it.

He shrugged himself forward off the wall, put his phone back into his pocket, and went back inside the Delphi. The swinging door to the men's room needed some oil; he noted it absently as he washed his hands in one of the sinks. Something else to do when the restrooms were renovated next week.

He looked at his face in the dust-specked mirror and saw that his eyes had dark shadows under them. That would be because he'd had another sleepless night, despite the fact that after Kitty had left yesterday he'd gone straight to the gym and spent two hours pedalling the exercise bike as fast as he could, and lifting heavier weights than he could safely handle. But although his body was exhausted, his mind, or his hormones, or his crotch, or wherever it was that his libido resided, wouldn't let him rest.

And now she wouldn't talk to him. And he had absolutely no idea what to do about it.

He should have some ideas. You couldn't be as intimate with as many women as Jack had been without learning something about the way they thought. But Kitty Giroux Clifford seemed determined to believe the worst of him.

He could go to her mother's house again and ask where she lived. But he'd gotten off on the wrong foot doing that the other night; Kitty had seemed prickly about him intruding on her privacy. And even if Mrs. Giroux did give him Kitty's address, and he turned up there and through some miracle she let him into her house, what would he do then?

He wouldn't be able to get anywhere near her until he made her trust him. He'd met plenty of suspicious women before, and usually he made them laugh. It put them off their guard. But Kitty hadn't laughed once when she was around him.

She thought he was a jerk.

"Aaaaaaaagh!" He clenched his fists and stormed out of the men's room and up the stairs to the cinema office. The room was closet-like, without windows or, at the moment, a telephone or a computer. The rickety desk was spread with Kitty's drawings. Jack flung himself into his chair and regarded them gloomily.

After mere minutes of sulking, he was drawn in. Jack lifted the nearest sheet and looked at it more closely. It was a detail of the concession stand, drawn with the missing tiles replaced, the counter refurbished in stainless steel and a chic minimalist light fixture replacing the bare bulb that hung there now. She'd captured the lines of what was there already and added something modern, clean and fresh.

It was exactly what he wanted, what he would have pictured if he'd had the skill himself. All of her drawings did that. They made his fantasy something that was doable. Here, within his grasp.

Unlike her.

He picked up another page, and another, and every single one of them carried with it that jolt of recognition, the feeling that here was his imagination made into reality. The woman was amazing. He'd been lucky to find her.

Or maybe he'd been unlucky. Was the incredible rush at seeing his dream for the Delphi come true worth the incredible frustration of not being able to touch her?

Maybe. Maybe not. Because now, following with his eyes the sweeps and curves her pencil made, he began to see her curves in there. The lines of the stage, long and elegant like her legs. The golden fruit decorating the cinema walls, deliciously rounded like her breasts. As if every part of the Delphi that she'd drawn had become her in some essential way.

He imagined her drawing these sketches. Narrowing those green eyes in concentration. Pushing her vibrant hair back from her face. Touching her pencil to her lips and taking the tip of it between them. As she'd taken him.

In his head, the pencil became his thumb between her lips two nights ago in the restaurant. He could feel the tentative touch of her tongue on his skin, then the smooth hardness of her teeth, the soft excitement of her lips surrounding him.

Jack groaned and laid his head on top of the stack of sketches. He had to do something. It surely wasn't healthy for a grown man to walk around in a more or less permanent state of arousal.

Okay. He'd tried the flirtatious, charming approach. He'd try being professional and distant. It was what she said she wanted. And maybe it would work.

After all, Jack had had a lot of practice at getting girls, and he'd learned not to rule any approach out. Ever since age fourteen, when the annoying giggling creatures he'd more or less ignored for years had suddenly become endlessly fascinating, he'd talked and laughed and kissed and touched and explored, and he was pretty good at it by now. Sooner or later, he'd discover something that would make Kitty go to bed with him.

He closed his eyes and sighed. Exhaustion weighed his limbs down.

For his sanity's sake, it had better be sooner.

"I want you more than I've ever wanted anyone. Anything."

This time he could see her, and this time he knew it was a dream.

Kitty's red hair was spread on the pillow underneath her head. Her green eyes smiled at him. Jack could feel the soft weight of her breasts in his hands as she lay beside him, one of her legs twined with his. His lips were still wet from her kiss. His tongue still tasted her sweetness.

Kitty's hand wrapped around his erection. Jack knew he'd waited such a long time for this, and he wanted her more badly than he'd ever thought possible. His flesh ached from wanting and waiting. And then she guided him into her, surrounded him with her warmth. Tight. Embracing. Sweet.

She brought his hand to her mouth, and he traced her smile with his fingers, and he couldn't look away from her eyes, so green.

This is the way it's supposed to be, he thought, and he began to move inside her. He took her hand and laid it on his lips, letting her fingers slip inside his mouth as his thumb had slipped inside hers. Everything was a kiss, perfect and arousing.

And then he heard a door open.

Jack sat bolt upright. He was at his desk, upstairs in the cinema office. The top sketch was crumpled slightly where he'd rested his head on it as he'd slept. And dreamed.

He ran his hands through his hair and shook his head to try to clear it.

No good. All he could see was Kitty lying beside him, looking into his eyes as he made love to her. His penis was achingly, throbbingly erect. And...he'd heard a door open. That was why he'd woken up.

Jack jumped up. It was Kitty; it had to be.

He paused halfway down the corridor. How had he decided to behave around Kitty? Distant and professional?

Was distant and professional possible with a rampant hard-on?

Jack shrugged and headed toward the stairs. Looked as if he was about to find out.

The Delphi's outer door creaked shut behind her and Kitty walked through the open inner door into the lobby, trying not to appear like a woman whose career was on the line.

If she was honest, worry about her career was only half the reason why her stomach felt like a jackrabbit who'd drunk three double espressos. But it was the only reason she was going to acknowledge to herself. Her feelings about Jack Taylor could take a running jump off a high cliff as far as she was concerned. She needed money. She needed a showcase for her talents. She was not going to let the Don Juan of Portland, Maine, play havoc with her hormones.

She'd spent her whole life unlucky. Left by her father, second-best at school, always second in line for promotion at her job. Dumped by her husband. And now, her high-school crush was making her jumpier than she'd been in years.

Well, she was going to break the pattern. She was going to keep control in this business relationship, at least.

"Hello?" she called into the semidarkness. Her voice echoed back to her faintly. The place needed curtains, she thought, to warm up the acoustics a little and break up the brown of the wood-panelled walls. Then she looked around and noticed: no windows. She'd obviously been in too much Jack-induced blind panic to notice during her other two visits.

"Better rethink that plan, then," she muttered, and then raised her voice. "Hello? Anyone here?"

"Hello, Katherine."

Her head swivelled to the left, and her stomach did another bunny-hop. Jack stood just inside an open door, on what she could see was the bottom step of a narrow wooden staircase. The white T-shirt he wore outlined the lean muscles in his upper arms and chest.

"I'm glad you could make it," he said. He wasn't smiling and his voice sounded detached; certainly without the flirtatiousness he'd used the other night.

But his eyes, somehow, smouldered. His cheeks were slightly flushed. He looked…aroused.

Kitty couldn't keep herself from looking down his body. The thick length of his penis was outlined clearly against the indigo denim of the crotch of his jeans.

Dear God, he was most definitely aroused.

"Come up to the office and let's talk." He turned and started up the staircase, and Kitty followed.

His voice and his body were telling two different stories. Why was he standing there, with a hard-on, speaking so coldly to her?

He was going to fire her from the job. He didn't like her sketches. Her jackrabbit stomach kicked with both legs, hard.

The thought of his erection didn't help; nor did the sight of his long legs and his backside, hugged by denim, ascending the stairs in front of her. *I don't think I've ever been so close to Jack Taylor's butt,* she thought dazedly as she climbed, *and I've known him for over thirteen years.*

It was a perfect butt. As if she didn't know already.

"The door on your left is the projection room," he said when they'd both reached the top. "Pretty basic, but functional, once I've got the projector fixed. I hope. My office is just down the corridor."

"Thanks." She walked behind him down the cramped, windowless passageway. Cobwebs clustered near the ceiling.

"I'm sorry it's so dingy. I don't think it's been cleaned since the seventies." He pushed a door on the left a little bit more open for her. "Please sit down. The chairs are clean, I promise." As she passed him she could feel heat radiating from his body. She was nearly close enough to touch him, and for a split second she thought her hip might brush against his arousal, but fortunately there was enough room for her, him and his erection in the doorway.

She tensed herself into the wooden chair closest to the door, and Jack walked around the desk and sat. The desk was spread with her sketches. The top one was her drawing of the concession stand. She'd liked it when she'd drawn it, but suddenly it looked amateurish and silly.

"So. Katherine. Thanks for bringing me your sketches. I've been looking at them."

If her stomach got any more jumpy she was going to throw up. The sooner she heard the bad news, the better. She could forget about her professional veneer, just for a minute. At least when he was sitting down she couldn't see his crotch.

"Do you want me to work for you?" she asked.

His eyebrows shot up, and his mouth opened slightly in surprise. She'd blown it. Kitty felt the familiar sickening heat of humiliation rush through her body. She lifted her hands to gather up her sketches and get the hell out of there before it got any worse.

"God, yes, I want you to work for me! You know exactly what I'm trying to achieve here. I love your ideas."

Kitty's hands stopped. She used one of them to wipe her forehead. Against all odds, she hadn't actually broken out in a sweat. "Good."

Good? She meant, *Great.* She meant, *Wicked awesome.* She meant *Thank You, Lord, for saving my business*. She mentally told her insides to settle down, and got to work.

"I'm excited about the project. Let me talk you through what I've given you here."

Jack leaned forward in his chair and she started to elaborate on some of her ideas. She could hear her own voice, brisk and professional, pointing out features and explaining the reasons behind her choices, but her mind was somewhere else. Traitor that it was, it was looking at Jack's strong hands spread out on the paper and remembering his thumbprint on her tongue. It was wondering whether his crotch felt like hers: hot, swollen, sensitive. Kitty finished talking about her idea of having a space in the lobby to feature work by young artists from the school of fine art up the street from the Delphi, and closed her eyes.

She had to stop thinking about Jack Taylor's body. Because if she thought about it for one second more she was going to reach forward and touch him. And if she touched him…

"What comes next?"

His question made her snap open her eyes. She trained them at the papers in front of her, determined not to think of what would come next if she let herself feel his skin. "I'd like to take some pictures of my own and ask you a few questions, if you've got time now. Then I'll start drawing up some more detailed plans."

"I've got time."

"Great. Let's do it." *Do it*? She stood, pulled her bag back onto her shoulder and walked back through the dusty hallway and down the stairs. *Business, Katherine*, she thought. She took her digital video recorder from her bag and switched it on. She didn't look to see whether he was still aroused. She didn't trust herself.

"Nice camera. I've never seen one so small. Latest model?"

She made a noncommittal sound and started recording the four walls of the lobby. Box office, concession stand, door up to the office and projection room on the left-hand wall. Heavy open doors to the vestibule on the front wall. Elegantly carved doors to the restrooms on the right wall, along with display space for film information. And the big doors to the light trap and the auditorium on the back wall.

"Your car is great, too," Jack added. "Must be fun to drive. Looks like your business is doing well."

She didn't even make a sound in response to that one. *Looked like* was right. "So what's your timescale for completion of the renovations?"

"Hmm. After falling through the trapdoor, I'm a little paranoid about the floor's safety. It seems to be okay, but I want to make sure I'm not going to get sued. We'll see what the engineers say."

He ticked off items on his fingers. "So get the floor checked out, some heating put in, I need the plumbing and the electricity modernized, we have to put in a telephone line so we can take bookings and get on the Internet, we need a new screen and a projector for the cinema, not to mention the chairs, which are a public health risk. Speaking of which, the restrooms need updating to twenty-first-century standards of hygiene. And I need to make sure we haven't got rats."

He looked at his hands, all ten fingers used up, and sighed and started again.

"Recarpeting, repainting, revarnishing of everything. I'm not sure about the roof, though from the damp stains upstairs I think it's going to need work. Oh, yeah, and I need to chisel the bricks out of the fire escape before I can open the doors to the general public. I'm guessing 2030. But I'm hoping within a year."

She wanted to laugh, but that would have required some relaxation of her body and mind. "Good luck," she said instead, and pushed open the heavy door to the light trap, and through to the theater itself.

Kitty was immediately reminded of what a wonderful space the Delphi was. The ceiling was twice as high as the lobby's, soaring up to those artificial beautiful stars, creating the wonderful illusion of an endless night sky. The room had such a feeling of history and promise. Even the musty air smelled like the fulfilment of some wonderful fantasy.

Kitty lifted her camera to her face and made a full circle. She caught Jack at the end of it, standing beside the last row of seats, stunning and half smiling in his indigo jeans and white T-shirt. Kitty pictured herself later, downloading the images onto her laptop in her makeshift office.

I am not going to scroll through it all until I get to the picture of Jack, she thought, though she knew she would. She would probably zoom it in on his crotch, too. God, she had a one-track mind.

"Are the chairs really a public health risk?" she asked, for something to say. She switched off her camera, flipped down the seat of the chair nearest to her, and perched the camera on it. The velvet was moldering, but the detail on the wooden arms was intact. She bent down to examine the mechanism that worked the seat. "Do you want to completely replace these, or simply reupholster them?"

Jack didn't reply. But she felt his hand, oh, no, like pure electricity, running its shocking palm up the side of her ribcage, to her shoulder, turning her around.

"Kitty," he said, and his voice was hoarse this time. His brown eyes burned into hers. "I can't ignore the way I feel about you, it's driving me crazy."

And then he pulled her into his arms and his mouth was covering hers.

Oh, no. Oh, yes. His hands buried themselves in her hair, holding her head to his, and to the incredible warmth of his lips. That mouth stayed pressed to hers for a heart-stopping moment while Kitty wondered what in the world she should do, and then his lips moved and she stopped thinking. Her hands found the back of his T-shirt and dug into the soft cotton, the firm muscles beneath. And she couldn't help it. She kissed him back.

Jack made a sound low in his throat and leaned closer. His kiss was hungry, demanding, open-mouthed, as if he wanted to devour her. She welcomed his tongue inside her mouth, the wonderful taste of him again, the heat that spread downward from where he touched her. Each urgent stroke of his tongue and lips made her crave more of him. Made her want to give him everything.

His hands tilted her head back and he trailed hot kisses down her neck. She felt his lips on the hollow of her throat, heard him inhale deeply and knew he was breathing in her scent. She shivered with the rightness of it, how wonderful it felt to have him taste her, breathe her, touch her.

Then his mouth was on hers again and his hands were on her hips, pulling her closer to him. At last she could feel the hard length of his arousal through their clothes, pressed against her stomach. Kitty arched into him and he groaned again.

"I need you," he muttered roughly against her mouth, and then tore his lips away from hers to pant hot, sweet words in her ear. "I can't stop thinking about you. Dreaming about you."

He captured her earlobe in his mouth, nipped softly at it with his teeth. A shiver of pleasure thrilled through Kitty's body.

"I want to touch you everywhere." Jack's hands roamed over her back, her shoulders, over her hips to cup her buttocks and crush her even tighter against him. "Do you want it, too?"

Yes. Please. Kitty tangled her fingers in his hair and answered him by bringing his mouth back to hers. Jack brushed her lips with his own, just touching her. And then slowly, so tantalizingly, he deepened the kiss. What had been a headlong plunge into passion became a leisurely exploration, and Kitty felt herself melting. Losing awareness of where they were, who she was, her entire being focused on the gentle movements of Jack's mouth and his hands holding her to him, the beat of his heart against her exquisitely sensitive breast.

"Oh, Kitty," he whispered between her lips, his breath slipping down her throat and into her, "it's going to be so good." Kitty moaned and gave herself up to Jack. His kiss was drugging. Overwhelming. Expert.

Expert.

Her mind suddenly started working again. Jack had kissed a lot of women. And the last time he'd kissed her, he'd been kissing someone else five minutes later.

Kitty planted her hands on Jack's chest and pushed him away, hard. He stumbled back a step and her body instantly demanded him again. The ache of unfulfilled desire, mixed with the dismay that had struck her with remembering the truth, made her feel faintly sick.

His face showed desire overcome by surprise. His hair tousled down over his forehead, disarrayed by her hands; his eyes were even darker than usual. "What's the matter?" he asked breathlessly.

"You're an extremely good kisser."

One eyebrow shot up. "That's a problem?"

She was dizzy, unable to catch her breath. She wiped the back of her hand across her mouth, trying to erase the burning feeling of Jack still there. "The problem is *why* you're such a good kisser."

He was still too close. Kitty retreated to the other side of the aisle, leaning against the arm of a chair.

"I don't understand," he said.

"How many women have you kissed, Jack? A hundred? Two hundred? A thousand?"

"So what? This is about you and me, not them."

His answer, implying that one of the huge figures she'd mentioned was at least close to correct, made her clench her fists in anger.

"It is about them, Jack. Because I'm one of them. One of the women you've kissed. One of the women you want to have sex with. Someone to add to your list before you move on to the next one." She headed toward the exit.

"Hold on. That's not fair." He caught up with her and grabbed her wrist so she had to stop. "Kitty, give me a chance here."

"How many chances have you already had, Jack? And with all those chances, how many times did you bother to see the real woman you were kissing? See how she felt, or what she thought, or who she was, or what you meant to her?" She wrenched her wrist away from him. "You don't deserve another chance."

He followed close behind her all the way across the lobby, through the vestibule and to the heavy outside door. She twisted the doorknob viciously. "Kitty—"

She turned, her hand still on the doorknob, the door just creaking open. "Our relationship is a professional one. Call me Katherine."

His brown eyes snapped. "You're being ridiculous. You want me as much as I want you, it's stupid to deny it. And I've changed since high school. You're wrong about me."

The freshness of the outside air cooled her face; sunlight dazzled her for a moment after the semidarkness of the cinema. She gulped in a breath, and then her eyes began to prick with tears as she realized how close she'd come to giving in to Jack Taylor. Losing her heart to him again.

And then, suffering the inevitable heartbreak. Again.

She swallowed hard, kept the tears at bay for a moment while she looked straight into Jack's eyes. He was angry. Well, that made sense. She didn't suppose many women turned him down. "I'm not wrong about you. You're exactly the same as you always were. And I'm not going to be another woman on your list."

Then she ran to her car, finally letting the tears stream down her cheeks once Jack could no longer see her face.

CHAPTER FIVE

KITTY'S anger lasted until the next morning, when the mailman delivered her bank statement. She stood in her bathrobe on her mom's worn-out doormat and stared at the piece of paper that told her that her savings were, finally, gone.

She leaned against the faded wallpaper in the hallway. What could she do? She could take out another business loan, but how would she repay it with no income? She could get a second job, but that would take her time away from promoting her own business. She could sell her car. But that was far, far too much like admitting she'd failed. Again.

She only had one choice, really. Kitty went upstairs to put on another designer suit.

The Delphi was already open when she got there; two big trucks had parked in front of the cinema and workmen were streaming out of the Delphi to the truck, carrying old sinks, rotten boards and rolls of carpeting. A whole other stream of workmen carried boxes, lengths of pipe, and, as Kitty watched, what looked like a urinal, into the building.

Kitty straightened her shoulders, held her portfolio high and proud and squeezed into the cinema, past a man in coveralls coming out. He winked at her and Kitty noticed what he was carrying: a cracked mirror. She refused to take it as an omen, and walked into the lobby.

The big room was full of people, but her eye unerringly picked out Jack as soon as she entered. He was deep in conversation with a man wearing a toolbelt. His face and gestures were animated; Kitty could see he was excited about what he was saying. She barely had time to register this, though, before he turned his head suddenly to look in her direction, and their eyes met.

Kitty nodded at him, not betraying the painful leap her heart made in her chest. Then she turned away and strode, as if she had every right in the world, through the double doors at the end of the room and into the theater itself.

It was emptier in here, though she spotted a couple of electricians examining the lights around the stage. She unzipped her portfolio and took out a sketch pad and pencil, all the while reminding herself of her game plan.

She was not going to let what kept on happening between her and Jack stop her from working on the Delphi. And she was not going to let it happen again. She was going to act confident of her own abilities. She'd choose to believe Jack had hired her for her skills, and not because he wanted to get her into bed. When Jack talked to her, she'd be calm and professional and proud and lay down some ground rules.

And then she'd hope like hell that Jack would follow them, because if he didn't cool down his approaches to her she was going to have to quit this job, and she quite simply couldn't afford to do that. She needed the money, and, more than that, she needed the success.

She'd only made a few notes about her thoughts for color schemes when she felt, rather than saw, Jack enter the room. God, it was like high school all over again, when she'd simply *known* whenever Jack had been near her. Marie had called it her "Special Taylor Sense". Kitty anchored her pencil in the curls at the back of her head and looked up at him.

Not going to beg for this job, she thought. She said, "I think the reds in here have faded a lot. I'd like to go for a deeper crimson on the seats and draperies to really offset the gilt. If you're happy with that, I'll source some fabric this afternoon."

Cool, controlled, professional, dignified. She liked it.

"That's great." Jack paused for a long time, looking steadily at her, his expression unreadable. She felt her dignity begin to melt, and she spoke again.

"Do you have any idea of when we can start some restoration work on the upholstery and décor in here?"

"The structural engineers are in the lobby now, and they're going to look in here in a minute. I'm hoping that this part is fairly sound, though I can't rule out dry rot. Looks like we'll need new wiring, but we can order in the light fixtures along with the sound system. As long as the walls and ceiling are okay we could start on the replastering and painting as soon as the wiring's done. Katherine, we need to talk."

His last comment was sudden enough to make her blink, but then she was back in her game plan. "Yes, Jack, we do. If we're going to work together, then—"

"We need to stop arguing. I agree."

"It's a little more complicated than that, Jack. You need to accept that I don't want a sexual relationship with you."

He folded his arms and leaned against the back of one of the chairs. "But it's even more complicated than that, Kitty. Because you *do* want a sexual relationship with me."

"I don't—"

He held up his hands. "You can argue all you want, but I was there when we kissed yesterday. And before that, in the restaurant. And when we saw each other for the first time again. It might be against your professional code, it might be against your better judgment, it might be against everything you think you know about me, but you want to have sex with me. And I want to have sex with you."

Kitty opened her mouth to reply, but her breathing seemed to have stopped.

Jack balled his hands into fists and rested them on his thighs. "Admit it. Please. For my sanity's sake, Kitty, please tell me that I'm right."

What was that expression in his eyes? It was almost like...desperation?

Kitty looked around the room. The electricians were engrossed in their work, way down the aisle.

"I'm not going to have sex with you."

"But you want to."

Want to? She wanted to so much she was totally scared to death. But what she wanted didn't stop there.

She wanted him to love her. Ten years after he'd broken her heart, she wanted to give it to him all over again. And that scared her even more.

"What I want is irrelevant to this job."

"But it's not irrelevant to me. Please just tell me, Kitty. And then we can move on. I'm not touching you, I'm not kissing you. I just need to know."

She took refuge from her pounding heart in sarcasm. "I'm a woman, Jack. Of course I want to have sex with you. Don't we all?"

He bit the inside of his lip and regarded her some more. "I'm not going to get a straighter answer than that from you, am I?"

"No."

After a long pause, he nodded. "Okay. I'll settle for that, for now. So what else do you want? How should I act around you? Can we be friends?"

Friends with Jack Taylor? Now that was a new concept. Kitty thought about how to respond to that one.

"I mean, we used to be friends, didn't we?" Jack continued. "Back in high school, in art class. We joked around. We had a good time. We liked each other. Before it all went wrong, we were friends."

Before it all went wrong. Try, *before you totally betrayed me*. But, Kitty had to admit, Jack was right. They had been friends.

"Okay," she said. "Friends is good."

Jack's face broke out in a smile. "Great. Excellent. We'll be friends."

"And we'll work on the Delphi together," she reminded him.

"Of course." The door into the theater opened, and Jack glanced over to it. "Speaking of which, here's the structural engineer. Come and talk to him, and he should give us an idea of what we can do next. Then," he said, leading her up the aisle toward the door, "we can discuss colors and fabrics in detail. Then we can go for a friendly drink or two, you can come to my house for a friendly dinner, and we can wind up the evening having friendly incredible sex with each other."

Kitty stopped dead in the aisle.

"Joke," said Jack, holding up his hands. "Joke. I'll respect your limits. I mean it."

She considered him, every muscle tensed, wondering, as always, how far to trust his sincerity.

And then she forced herself to relax. The job was the important thing, wasn't it? And if she was going to second-guess everything Jack said, if she was going to expect him to violate their agreement from the moment they made it, then there was no way she was going to be able to do the job.

She'd have to trust him. For now.

So she smiled and said, "See that you do respect my limits, Mr. Taylor. Or else I might have to lock you up in a cell somewhere."

"Mmm. Always did like prison movies. *The Shawshank Redemption*. *Cool Hand Luke*. Not usually enough women in them, though. Come and meet Stuart, the engineer. The guy who's with him is Dave, the construction foreman. Stuart, Dave, I'd like you to meet Katherine Clifford, who's doing the Delphi's interior design."

Kitty shook hands with both men.

"I want you two and Katherine to talk directly to each other whenever you need to. She's a fantastic designer and, Dave, whatever she asks you to do is okay with me. Katherine's the boss."

He was talking to the men, but Kitty caught the meaning for her underneath his words. He had faith in her skill as a designer. And he intended to keep their personal relationship within the limits she'd imposed. She could trust him.

Now all she had to worry about was how much she could trust herself.

"That's the Little Dipper done. Next…looks like Cassiopeia."

Kitty checked her photograph of the original ceiling again to make sure she had chosen the right spot to put the next star. She stuck a stencil to the smooth midnight blue paint of the ceiling and began to apply the thin coating of sticky adhesive.

She glanced across the scaffolding to where Jack sat, filling in blue paint around the decorative edges of the ceiling. "Do you know anything about astronomy?"

"Only what I've learned from seeing science fiction movies," he answered, his eyes intent on his work. "Why do you ask?"

"I was just wondering if this ceiling is anything like the real night sky. If the constellations are in the right place."

"I don't think it matters," Jack said, dabbing his brush into a crevice. "People don't go into a cinema to see real life. They go in wanting to live a dream. Better than life."

"Sounds like you know what you're talking about."

"I know all about dreams," said Jack. "Believe me. I've had some important ones."

She applied two more stencils, sketching out half of a "W" shape. "The Delphi's your dream, isn't it?" she asked. "You've wanted to do this for a very long time."

"Ever since I was a kid. I came in here a couple times when I was a teenager."

Kitty burst into laughter. "When it was a porn theater? You're disgusting."

"I didn't see a movie. Well, not a whole one anyway. I pretended to be eighteen when I was fifteen and tried to get a job at the concession stand. I didn't get the job but I snuck into the theater after the interview. I couldn't believe how beautiful it was."

"What, the room or the porn movie?" Kitty giggled.

"The room, of course. I remember seeing the stars on the ceiling first, before anything else. That's probably not true, because it was dark and I was probably looking where I was going, but that's what I remember. The stars."

As she listened Kitty lifted a trembling sheet of silver leaf, holding it lightly by the edges, and pressed it gently into place. She stroked it onto the sticky surface with a soft brush, and then slowly removed the stencil and rubbed the extra leaf away with a silk cloth, polishing the silver. Even close up, the star shone.

"Then, of course, I saw the porn movie that was playing. Which was a life-changing experience in itself. I never knew that people could bend that way."

Kitty clapped her hand to her mouth so her laughter wouldn't scatter the silver leaf sheets all over the scaffolding.

"Needless to say, I was disgusted and left immediately," Jack said.

"Needless to say." She moved over to the next stencil. "And that's when you decided you wanted to own the Delphi."

"Yeah. Not because of the porn. Because of the stars. And what this place could be."

Exactly how had this happened? Kitty wondered as she held her breath and lifted another delicate silver leaf. When had she begun to feel comfortable around Jack Taylor? Able to carry on a normal conversation, to work side by side, to joke around, without feeling tongue-tied or angry or nervous or frightened?

It had crept up on her. It had been seven weeks, nearly eight, since she and Jack had agreed to be friends. Gradually, as they had worked together, the cinema had begun to look less like a dusty ghost of what it once had been, and more like something that could be wonderful and real. And she had felt less and less like a bundle of raw nerves and emotions, and more like herself.

And it had become easy to be with Jack. It had become fun. He joked around with the electricians, engineers and carpenters. He was totally serious about the renovation, but his enthusiasm was so infectious that it didn't feel as if they were all working; it felt as if they were creating something together. And along with the new lighting and the new plaster and the new tiling in the restrooms, Kitty and Jack had, somehow, created a new camaraderie.

It was like this in high school art class, thought Kitty as she worked her way across the night-blue expanse of ceiling toward where Jack sat painting around the golden plaster roses. In the moments when she'd been able to forget her huge teenage crush and relax around Jack, they'd been friends.

Just in that one class, just for those few months, of course. She was a year younger and Jack had been the most popular kid in the school. She would've never had the confidence to sit at his table at lunch, for example. She never even would have been friends with him at all if he hadn't suddenly noticed her, one day in art class, when she'd been lost in a fantasy world of her own.

"So what did you dream about when you were fifteen?" asked Jack.

Besides you?

"I wanted to be an artist. I wanted to create something that was beautiful and meaningful at the same time."

"Sort of like these stars?"

She stopped, mid-polish.

"Yes. Sort of like these stars."

Kitty looked at Jack at exactly the same moment that Jack looked at Kitty. Their eyes met and it was a shock, an intense pleasure and an intense longing at the same time.

Kitty felt her fingers loosening on the cloth and knew she was going to drop it, but she couldn't look away. His eyes were deep brown and they made her feel, as always, as if he were touching her. But her longing was more than sexual. It had something more to do with talking with him and working with him and sharing laughter and a past.

Though it felt like a physical wrenching, she turned her head away and looked at the ceiling instead of Jack. "I think you should do a few of these stars," she said. She was good at applying silver leaf, she'd done a lot of it through the years and on this ceiling, but her hands felt suddenly far too unsteady.

"No, thanks. You're doing a great job." Jack's voice was quiet.

"But it's your cinema. It's your dream. They're your stars."

"It's your dream now. Your stars."

He spoke seriously, and Kitty had to catch her breath at his words, because they were true. The Delphi had become her dream, too.

No, no, no, all wrong, she thought. She didn't have dreams. She lived in the real world. Dreaming was just setting yourself up for disappointment.

Suddenly, she wanted their previous joking tone back again. "You've got to do some stars. You can't let all your artistic talent go to waste on painting walls."

"Kitty, I have no artistic talent, remember? I suck at art. I'll stick to this mindless coloring in, thanks."

"Don't be silly; you don't suck. Come on, get up and come over here. You can do Perseus." She held out a stencil to him.

He was smiling now. He put down his paint, and rose. "All right, but you have to help me."

Kitty had a sudden vision of holding Jack's hand, guiding it, standing leaning against him, and she felt her pulse speed up. "I'll just tell you how to do it and you can do it yourself."

"I'll mess it up," he warned her, taking the stencil. "I'll ruin the ceiling and you'll have to do the whole thing again."

"We're really high up here, Jack. Nobody's going to be able to see it if you make a mistake. Okay, put the first one here." She laid her finger on the cool blue plaster, and watched as Jack painstakingly stuck the stencil to the ceiling.

She wasn't touching him. But he was close enough for her to be able to hear his soft breathing and the rustle of his clothes, and to smell his warm scent. If she turned around, she could be in his arms in a split second.

Kitty had been on this scaffold, far above the ground, for hours at a time and she had never felt the height. She'd never felt dizzy or scared or shaky.

But now, with Jack so close to her, Kitty felt vertigo. As if she were perched on a high cliff, and she had an irresistible attraction to the edge. And if she let herself come any nearer, she would start to fall.

"Now put a thin layer of this adhesive on the plaster." She held out the container to him. As he took it, his fingertips brushed hers.

"So it's Memorial Day this weekend," she said, hoping mundanities would distract her from the bad, wonderful things her body was doing to her. "Do you have any plans?"

"A long cycle ride down the coast, if the weather's okay," Jack replied, brushing the adhesive onto the plaster. "I'll stay overnight somewhere. Want to join me?"

Mundanities didn't help. She still felt close to the edge. "Can't, thanks. My family is having a big barbecue on Saturday afternoon. My brother Nick's coming down from Mount Desert Island, and we've got about a million relatives."

Jack finished with the stencil. "Okay, what's next?"

"You can put leaf on one of the ones I've already done where the adhesive has dried enough. Here, lift one of these sheets, very carefully, from the edges." She held out the book of silver leaf to him.

Jack shook his head. "No way, that looks too delicate. I'll tear it."

"It's okay. If you tear it, we can patch it. Besides, you're paying for the stuff. Just be careful."

"All right, but if I mess this up—"

"Oh, and I forgot to say, don't breathe, or you'll make it fly away."

She held her breath, too. Jack leaned forward, close enough for her to feel the warmth from him, and lifted the precious trembling leaf with his fingertips.

"How am I doing?" he murmured, and she knew he wasn't talking about the silver leaf, but about something just as delicate, and maybe even more precious.

She held her finger to her lips to quiet him, and showed him with motions how to lay the leaf gently against the sticky adhesive. He wrinkled it a little getting it on, and turned to her with dismay on his face.

"Told you I'm bad at this," he whispered, but she shook her head and handed him the brush to press the leaf into the stencil.

It wouldn't hurt just to help him. To guide his hand a little bit. She hadn't touched him in weeks now, and, while that was a good thing, because it let them be friends, she'd craved it so much.

She put her hand on his wrist. She heard his sharp intake of breath, felt his hot skin and the strong, fast pulse beneath it.

"Just be gentle, and you'll be fine," she whispered.

"Show me." His voice was low and deep, and stirred the curls on her neck. "Show me what you want."

"Mr. Taylor?"

A female voice drifted up to them from below. Jack and Kitty both started, and Kitty dropped her hand. They went to the side of the scaffolding to peer down. A slender blond woman stood in the aisle of the cinema, looking up.

"Hi," Jack called down. "I'm Jack Taylor."

"I'm Lily Grace, from the *Portland Times*. I made an appointment with you to do an interview about the cinema restoration?"

"Oh. Great. Okay, I'll be right down."

Jack gave Kitty the brush. "You'll have to finish Perseus, I guess. I'm sorry we were interrupted."

Was she sorry?

Kitty took the brush and watched Jack climb down the ladder to the floor, where the blonde waited for him. She was young and, Kitty saw, very attractive. She wore a skirt that skimmed her thighs and a blouse that showed quite a bit of cleavage, from this vantage point.

Jack reached the ground and shook hands with the woman. "Come down near the stage, Miss Grace. I've got a clean chair down there somewhere."

"Call me Lily," was the last thing Kitty could hear clearly before the two of them walked down the aisle to the front of the cinema.

She felt something sick stab at her stomach. Oh, she knew what was coming next. Jack Taylor, master flirt, at work. No member of the female species safe. She turned her back resolutely and went to work finishing up Perseus.

Silver-leafing stars was absorbing. Silver-leafing stars took all of her attention. Getting everything right, completely faithful to the photograph she had of the original ceiling. She was going to produce the best damn ceiling ever, practically the Sistine Chapel of Portland, Maine, and to do that she needed every bit of concentration she could muster.

She managed three stars before she peered over the edge.

Jack was sitting on the stage, with the woman in a folding metal chair in front of him. He was talking animatedly, gesturing with his hands, pointing at various features of the room. Lily Grace was nodding and writing in a notebook.

He wasn't obviously flirting with her. Kitty didn't detect any lingering eye contact. And from where they were sitting at the moment, they couldn't touch each other.

But Jack didn't need glances or touches to flirt with a

woman. He could do it just by being himself. He could do it just by holding a trembling leaf of silver, for God's sake.

Kitty went back to the ceiling. In two minutes, she checked on Jack again.

He still wasn't flirting.

She forced herself to hold her hands steady, and hold her breath while she smoothed another silver star.

Her emotions and her libido were a total wreck. But these stars, at least, were going to be perfect.

"It was wonderful to meet you, Jack. Here's my card, in case you want to get in touch. About anything. My home number's on the back."

Jack took the business card from Lily and put it in his back pocket without looking at it. "Thanks, Lily. I'll look forward to your article."

He closed the Delphi's door after her and leaned his forehead against its cool surface.

"You look like a man who needs some good news."

Jack answered Oz without moving his head. "I need more than good news, Oz. I need some reverse Viagra, something to kill off my sex drive completely. Or a miracle."

"I see what you mean. That blond reporter was hot. I saw her when she came in."

"You like her? Here's her number." Jack pulled the card out of his pocket and handed it to Oz. "I was talking about Kitty."

Oz examined the card closely and then put it in his own pocket. "I thought you said that things were going well with Kitty."

"I was exaggerating." He turned around and leaned back against the door. "I meant that things were going relatively well. I decided to be friends with her to stop her hating me, and I think that's working. But I can't think of anything but her. I'm surrounded by professionals here at the Delphi, which is good because I keep on making stupid mistakes. I keep losing things, like my keys. I lost my cell phone somewhere today, or maybe yesterday. I don't know anymore. I think I might be going crazy."

"'Crazy' is also perhaps exaggerating. I see mentally disordered people on a fairly regular basis and, although you're far from normal, I wouldn't class you with the mentally ill just yet. Even if you have lost your phone."

Jack hauled in a deep breath. "I mean it, Oz. Every time I'm around her I'm hyper-aware. Every single thing she does turns me on, and I can't show it. You remember the John Cusack character in *The Sure Thing*, who had to hitchhike across America with this girl he really liked and share a bed with her and everything, and couldn't ever touch her? Like that."

"That's maddening," Oz agreed.

"Or the John Cusack character in *Grosse Pointe Blank*, remember the one who had recurrent dreams about his high-school prom date and when he saw her again she wouldn't let him touch her because he was a hit man?"

"I see what you mean," said Oz. "You're not a hitchhiking hit man, though. And you don't really look like John Cusack."

Jack ran his hands through his dark hair. "You're not helping, you know."

"Hey." Oz gripped Jack's shoulder. "Hey, buddy, I'm sorry. Listen, I've got some good news. The restrooms are all finished. And come with me. I've got something to show you. Just to prove I'm confident that your relationship with Kitty will work out the way you want it to."

"Is this what you've been chuckling about for days?" Jack asked, and followed Oz through the inner doors, across the lobby and into the men's room.

His attention immediately focused on a new, gleaming white vending machine on the freshly tiled wall.

"You've installed a condom machine," he said.

"Yup. Fully stocked. Flavored, colored, ribbed for her pleasure. There should even be some plain ones in there. I'm sure you have enough of them at home, but it never hurts to be prepared wherever you are."

Jack looked from the condom machine to his friend, his frustration forgotten, his lips curving into a grin. "I'm touched by the show of faith. Thank you."

"Hey, no problem. It's a business venture. I'll expect a share in the condom-related profits when the Delphi is up and running. And I'll expect you to buy me a beer for every one of them that you personally use."

"It's a deal." They shook hands. "I think you're going to be thirsty for quite a while, though."

"You can buy me a beer now on spec," Oz said as they walked out to the lobby.

"Sure. If Kitty doesn't need me to finish painting. Hey!" He snapped his fingers. "Your confidence in me has given me an idea."

"What's that?"

"All this friendship stuff is frustrating, but it means I'm getting to know Kitty better. She said her family is having a big barbecue on Saturday. What if I dropped by there, just to say hi, and got to know her family? That would help us get closer, right?"

Oz considered. "I'm not sure about this, Jack. Kitty seems to be an intensely private person. She might not welcome you barging into her personal life."

"We talked about our dreams today, Oz. She told me what it was she wanted the most in the world. Does that sound like someone who doesn't want me barging into her personal life?"

"Well, no, but—"

"Exactly. We've proven we can work together and get along. I should get to know her better, as a person. If she knows I don't just want her for sex, she'll be more likely to have sex with me. Right?"

Slowly, Oz shook his head. "Somehow I find that logic less than convincing."

"Don't worry, Oz. I have a good feeling about this."

CHAPTER SIX

"HEY Kit, Mom tells me you've got a new boyfriend," Nick said, turning the chicken on the grill.

Kitty nearly dropped the bowl of barbecue sauce she'd been about to hand to her brother. "Mom is wrong. I don't have a new boyfriend."

"So who's the guy with the bike, talking with Mom?"

Oh, no.

Jack Taylor, tall and tanned and gorgeous, wheeling his bicycle across their lawn, walking next to her mother. Smiling. Saying something she couldn't hear. Coming closer. The bowl tilted in Kitty's suddenly numb hands, and a glob of bright red sauce fell onto her white capris.

"What on earth is he doing here?" she gasped.

"Getting invited to dinner, it looks like," Nick answered. "You going to save some of that barbecue sauce for the chicken, or should I put you on the grill instead?"

Kitty felt as if she were on the grill already. She put down the bowl and wiped her capris with a paper towel, utterly failing to remove the stain. "Stupid bad luck," she muttered, walking rapidly toward Jack and her mother. Spicy mesquite. Her favorite perfume.

Jack caught her eye and waved. She walked faster, trying to cover the stain with one hand.

"Hi, Kitty!" he called.

"Hi, Jack. Why are you here?"

"Jack was going for a bike ride and happened to be in the neighborhood," Sue Giroux piped up. "I was just saying we have enough food for an army, so he should stay for something to eat."

"I'm sure Jack is really busy, Mom."

"No, I haven't got any plans. That chicken smells great, Mrs. Giroux." Jack smiled. He had such a beautiful smile. A beautiful, confident, maddening smile.

"Mom, can I talk to you for a minute?"

Kitty grabbed her mother's arm and pulled her to one side, out of Jack's earshot. "I don't want Jack to come to the barbecue," she whispered.

"Why not? You need a new man in your life, after Sam."

"Not this man, Mom."

Sue patted her arm. "Sam was good-looking, but he was dull. Jack seems more exciting. Did you see him smiling when he saw you just now?"

"Yeah, he was probably laughing because I look like an extra in a horror movie." She gestured at her red-spattered capris.

Sue waved her hand dismissively. "You can change your pants. Don't be so pessimistic, Kitty. This will be fun."

"It won't be fun!" she cried in desperation, and then quickly lowered her voice. "I don't want Jack to find out I'm living at home. I don't want him to know that I had to give up my office and that I haven't got any other work."

She glanced over at Jack. He'd propped his bike up against a tree and was shaking hands with her cousin Raymond. Cousin Raymond, who'd had a few beers already and was bound to start blurting out family secrets any second.

"Why don't you want him to know this stuff?" Sue asked, furrowing her forehead.

"Because I want him to think I'm successful."

"But you are successful, honey. You said the Delphi was going really well."

"Yes, but nothing else is."

Sue reached up and smoothed locks of Kitty's hair back behind her ears, a familiar gesture that made Kitty feel all of five years old. "You should be truthful with people, sweetheart. That's the only basis for a relationship."

"But Jack and I don't have a relationship!"

Sue just squeezed her shoulder and turned back to Jack. Kitty, hurrying alongside her mother, pulled her locks of hair loose again.

"You might not think you have a relationship yet," Sue said. "But there's definitely something there. The minute you spotted Jack, you came to life. I've never seen you looking more alive."

Kitty stopped. Her heart was pounding; she was panting; she felt as if every square inch of skin was flushed and tingling. Colors seemed sharper, scents were stronger and she could sense each movement Jack made without even looking at him.

Her mother was right. She'd never felt more alive. And it happened every single time she was with Jack.

Damn him.

"I'll admit there's an ulterior motive for me coming by today," Jack was saying to her mother as Kitty approached them. He caught her eye again, and winked subtly.

Ulterior motive. Would that be flirting with me, trying to drive me absolutely insane, or both?

Jack opened up one of the saddlebags on his bike and pulled out a folded newspaper. "I don't know if you've read today's *Times* already. There's something on the front of section two you might be interested in." He opened the paper and handed it to Sue.

"THE DELPHI RISES FROM THE ASHES," Kitty read over her mother's shoulder. The article covered the entire page and had two large color photographs. One was of Jack, standing on a ladder outside the cinema, smiling and screwing a new lightbulb into the big art deco DELPHI sign. The second was of the midnight-blue ceiling with all of Kitty's shining silver stars.

"There'll soon be a new star in Portland's sky, when visionary entrepreneur Jack Taylor opens the doors to his spectacular renovation of the Delphi Theater," read Sue, aloud.

"Look at this paragraph." Jack pointed, and Sue read.

"Taylor is enthusiastic in showing off the new innovations of the Delphi alongside the painstaking restoration of period features. 'I've been working with Katherine Clifford, a new local interior designer, and she's amazing,' he says, pointing out the cleverly concealed lighting system in the cinema, which enhances the art deco styling around the screen. The cinema is a testament to Taylor and Clifford's love of detail; every inch of the interior that has been restored is true to the 1920s origin of the building, while incorporating modern comfort."

Sue turned to Kitty, her eyes shining. "Oh, sweetheart, that's wonderful."

"Yes, it is." Her voice was quiet, and she felt Jack watching her. So while she'd been trying to catch him flirting with the leggy blond reporter, he'd been singing her praises instead. She lifted her eyes to his: dark pools of chocolate, warm and sweet.

"Thank you," she said.

"There's nothing to thank me for. It's the truth."

"Hey," piped up cousin Raymond, "that's wicked awesome. That calls for another beer." He wandered off. In a remote corner of her mind, Kitty knew she should be relieved. But she was too busy feeling meltingly alive.

"We're doing this together, Kitty," Jack said, and his voice was as seductive and wonderful as his eyes. "We're really building something incredible."

"Yes," Kitty replied, and she wasn't sure whether she was

talking about the Delphi, or about something else that was building up between them. Something that was becoming more irresistible by the second. Her gaze dropped from Jack's eyes to his mouth, and her own lips parted as she remembered the searing pleasure of his kiss.

"This publicity is going to be a real boost for your career," Sue said. "I bet the calls will come flooding in now."

Kitty stiffened as reality came back all in a rush. Her truth-loving mother was going to let Jack know just how desperate she was for some success.

And Kitty had vowed never, ever, to look desperate in front of Jack Taylor again.

"Well, publicity is always welcome," she said lightly, giving her mother the evil eye.

"It's a great article," Jack agreed. "I brought along something else to help us celebrate it. If you don't mind." He reached back into his saddlebag and pulled out a bottle of champagne. Vintage, Kitty noticed.

Sue led them to the picnic table, laden with salads and Kool-Aid and plates and glasses. Jack popped open the champagne's cork, and her relatives gathered around to watch as he poured the frothing liquid into the glasses Sue gave him. The glasses had cartoon characters on their sides, Kitty noticed; her mother had got them free from a gas station some time back in the eighties.

Kitty thought about the crystal champagne flutes she'd been given for her wedding to Sam. They'd been perfect. In fact, her entire house had been perfect. She'd decorated all of it herself. It had been exactly the type of house she'd wanted to have when she was growing up: elegant, sophisticated, tasteful. Completely opposite to the house she actually had grown up in, with its shabby furniture held together by duct tape.

She'd always believed appearances were important. She was an interior designer and she'd always wanted the best. But her perfect house hadn't been able to stop her marriage from crumbling. And her mother's house was held together with love, not with duct tape.

Jack gave her a glass of champagne. It had the Road Runner on it. She clinked it with his and with her mother's and with her family's, and the sparkling wine tasted like success to her.

"So are you going to introduce me, or what?"

Her brother's voice startled her out of her thoughts. "Oh. Right, sure," she said. "Jack, this is Nick Giroux, my younger brother. Nick, this is Jack Taylor. He owns the cinema I'm working on."

Nick put out his hand for Jack to shake, and as Jack took it Kitty nearly stumbled backwards.

It was a day for strange revelations. First, the knowledge that what was between her and Jack was so obvious that her relatives could see it. Then the article, and the idea that Jack thought her work was amazing. Then the realization that maybe merely projecting an image of success wasn't as important as she'd always thought.

And now, the fact that her brother, Nick, as he shook Jack's hand, looked exactly like a younger version of their father.

She'd always thought of Nick as a kid, but suddenly he looked like a full-grown man. He had the same broad shoulders, the same height, the same thick chestnut hair that her father had had the last time Kitty had seen him.

She had been thirteen. Nicky had been ten. And even though she'd never seen her father since the day he'd left, the sudden illusion that two of the men in her life who'd betrayed her were standing in front of her shaking hands made her eyes sting and her breath catch in her throat.

"I remember you," Nick was saying, and his voice shattered the illusion. He sounded like himself, her beloved, impetuous, noble little brother, who'd rescued every sick kitten and every injured seagull in Portland, in order to prove in his own way that he wasn't like a father who would abandon his family.

She drew in a shaky breath of relief. And then realized that she was still in trouble.

Nick knew all about the prom incident. And his voice sounded more like a protective brother's than a noble kitten-rescuer's.

"I'm sorry, I don't think we've ever met," Jack said.

Nick still gripped Jack's hand, and his eyes met Jack's in a challenge. "The only reason we never met was because Kitty physically held me back. I was all set to punch your lights out after what you did to her at the prom. But Kitty wouldn't let me."

Kitty launched into action. "Nick," she said, pulling on her brother's sleeve, "I think the grill needs your attention. Jack, let's go for a walk around the block."

The moment Nick had reluctantly turned away, Kitty was striding across the lawn in the opposite direction. Jack jogged up behind her, and then kept pace.

"That was awkward for a minute," Jack said. "Why'd you take off all of a sudden?"

"I didn't really want to see what was going to happen. The last time I stopped Nick punching you he was fourteen. He's grown a little bit since then."

"You didn't need to break it up, you know. I could have explained."

"Explained what? Why he shouldn't punch you? Because believe me, the only reason I stopped Nick from hitting you all those years ago was because you were four years older and bigger than he was. It wasn't because you didn't deserve to be hit."

"Okay." Jack stopped in the middle of the road. "I thought we'd gotten over this, but it looks like we haven't. Are you still mad at me? For something that happened ten years ago? Is this why you don't like me turning up at your barbecue? Is this the reason why you don't want to go to bed with me?"

"The reason I don't want to go to bed with you," Kitty shot back, "is because I have no desire to be another notch on your bedpost."

"And the reason you think I keep notches on my bedpost is because I had a lot of girlfriends in high school."

"And since high school, Jack. Be honest."

"Okay. And since high school. You're right. I like women. I like sex. But the reason you think I'm a cheat and a liar is because of what happened on prom night ten years ago. And that really is not fair. It wasn't that big a deal, Kitty."

Kitty felt as if she'd been hit herself.

"Not that big a deal?" she gasped.

"No. We were friends, we went to a dance together, I went and kissed someone else, you got mad. That's what happened, right?"

"Wrong. Look, Jack. Sit down." She pointed to a bench on the side of the road. "We need to talk this through, because I think you remember this differently than how I do."

And because suddenly, even though she'd tried to hide her life from Jack, she wanted him to know the truth about the past. Just how much he had hurt her.

Jack sat down, crossed his arms and looked at her expectantly. "Okay, Kitty. Refresh my memory. Tell me about prom night from your point of view."

"It didn't start on prom night," Kitty said. "It started when I was thirteen and my father left us. He went hunting one weekend and he never came back. He called from somewhere in New Hampshire to tell us he was all right, and every now and then we'd get a postcard. But I never saw him again."

Jack's forehead furrowed. "I'm sorry about that, Kitty. That must've been hard for you and your family. But I don't see what it has to do with me."

"It has to do with you because I was a sad and lonely teenager. I was desperate to find somebody to love. And that somebody was you."

Kitty sat down on the arm of the bench, a careful distance away from Jack. Her cheeks felt violently hot. Until today, she'd have died rather than tell Jack this. But she had to. Otherwise he wouldn't understand the full extent of how he had affected her, how he had changed her teenage life completely with a series of careless gestures.

Even though she knew it wouldn't make the slightest bit of difference to Jack, she wanted him to understand. And she wanted to remind herself why she couldn't let herself be hurt by Jack Taylor again.

"I had a crush on you since the second day of my freshman year," she said. "I stood behind you in the lunch line and heard you joking with the cafeteria ladies, and you laughed and I fell in love with you. You had two pieces of pizza, some green beans and three cartons of milk. You were wearing jeans and a red T-shirt.

"My best friend Marie and I sat at the table next to you. I only had yogurt for lunch because I'd had my braces tightened the day before and my mouth hurt, but I couldn't eat anything anyway, because I couldn't stop looking at you.

"For weeks, whenever I saw you again in the hallway or the cafeteria, my mouth would start to ache. Like my teeth were reminding me how it felt to fall in love with you."

"Wow." Jack's voice was serious. "I'm amazed you remember all this."

"Obviously you've never had a crush on anyone."

He didn't reply. Despite herself, she looked at him, and was surprised by what she saw. He was staring at her, biting the inside of his lip, and he was evidently deep in thought.

"No," he said slowly, "I don't think I ever have before."

His face was normally so animated. But now it was still and intense, in a way that she'd only seen a few times before. In the restaurant, when he'd been telling her about his plans for the Delphi. And on the scaffolding, when they'd talked about dreams.

It was a different side of Jack Taylor: thoughtful, serious, passionate.

She hurried on.

"I had a major crush on you for nearly three years even though I never talked to you. And then in my junior year we were in the same art class together, and I still didn't have the courage to talk with you. Until one day you came up behind me and saw I was drawing a picture of you."

She remembered it as vividly as if no time had passed: the cataclysmic moment when Jack Taylor had looked over her shoulder and seen the evidence of how much she worshipped him, black and white in charcoal on paper.

"It was a good picture," Jack said. "I was flattered."

Kitty shook her head. "I thought I was going to die. But you were—nice. You asked me to help you draw. You made me feel important."

"Hey, you were darn important. You helped me pass that class. I've always been crap at art." Jack's voice was light again, good-natured, exactly the opposite of how she felt. "And we had fun, didn't we?"

"Yes. You kept on teasing me about not having seen any films."

"You still haven't. There should be a law against it."

She stared at a tree across the road and forced herself to go on.

"And one day we were talking about the prom. I was on the decorating committee, and I asked you who you were going with. You always had a date for everything. But you said you hadn't asked anybody yet, and I sort of blurted out did you want to go with me."

She remembered the moment when he'd smiled and said yes. The fear as soon as she'd asked, and then the joy that had been so overwhelming that it had felt like pain.

She turned suddenly to Jack. "Why did you say yes? You could have gone with any girl in the school."

"You were cute. I liked you. I thought it would be fun. I didn't know I'd still be paying for it ten years later."

In a funny way, although it infuriated her that he wasn't taking her story seriously, Jack being flippant made it easier for Kitty than it had been five minutes ago, when he'd been so thoughtful. Flippant was the way she expected him to be. She knew how to deal with that. She stood up, and walked back and forth on the sidewalk in front of Jack.

"I'm sure you don't want to hear about how long it took me to find the perfect dress and how I used most of my savings from my job at Shop 'n' Save to pay for it. Or how I tried it on every night beforehand and dreamed about being with you. You went with me on a whim, and it wasn't important to you.

"But for me, that night was the most romantic moment of my life. I'd been in love with you for years, and here I was, on your arm, your date."

Though the gym had been decorated with streamers and balloons, it had still smelled of old rubber and sweat. None of that had mattered to Kitty, her hated red hair tamed into an elegant upsweep, her feet pinched by the highest-heeled shoes she'd ever worn. She'd been in heaven. Walking on clouds. Dancing on rainbows. The teenage heroine of her own romance novel, on the way to her happily-ever-after with Jack Taylor, the cutest boy in all of Portland High.

"And then we danced to a slow dance and you kissed me," she said.

"Yes. I kissed my prom date, because I wanted to." He sounded fed up. "And then you went to get a glass of punch and when you came back I was on the dance floor making out with Melissa Beauchamp."

"Rhymes with 'tramp'."

"But she kissed *me*, Kitty. She came up to me on the dance floor and sort of grabbed me."

"I saw," Kitty said, quietly.

She'd been walking back to the dance floor and seen

Melissa Beauchamp, the girl with the worst reputation in the school, walking toward Jack. She'd been wearing a bright green dress too small for her breasts. Melissa had approached Jack like a spearmint piranha. Put her arms around his neck and flashed a big, toothy, lip-glossed smile at him.

Kitty had actually giggled to herself. *He's here with me,* she'd thought. *He doesn't want you, Melissa.*

Jack had looked surprised to see Melissa draped all over him. And then he'd smiled back at her, and put his arms around her waist.

"You didn't push her away," Kitty said. "I thought you'd say no to her. And you didn't."

Jack looked away from her. He studied the tree across the road that she'd been staring at earlier.

"You took me to the prom and then you dumped me for the easiest girl in the school," Kitty said. "Was it worth it, Jack? Was she a good kisser? Did you get to have sex with her?"

Jack winced. "No. I—we didn't."

It was stupid, but she felt relieved to hear that he hadn't. Ten years ago, her imagination had been going crazy.

"So why did you kiss her?"

Jack screwed his eyes shut. "She kissed me. It just sort of happened. What do you want me to say?"

"See?" Kitty threw her hands up in the air. "And you wonder why I've hated you for ten years. It's not exactly Prince Charming behavior, is it?"

"I was eighteen," Jack said. "I was just a kid. I didn't know how to behave. I tried to apologize to you afterwards. I tried a lot, actually. You didn't want to hear it."

Kitty clenched her fists. "Because I was seventeen and everybody at school knew about what you'd done to me, and I felt like a total loser!"

Her words echoed in her ears, and she heard the pain and anger in them. All at once, Kitty saw how much her feelings had regressed ten years, back to the summer of her junior year in high school.

For a moment, she saw the whole thing as an outsider would, how Jack probably did. How trivial it would all seem. A teenage crush gone wrong, another ugly duckling abandoned for the swan in the skintight prom dress.

And then Jack said the words that were in her mind.

"Kitty, come on. Don't you think it's a little extreme to hate me for something I did ten years ago when we were both kids?"

The words, from Jack's mouth, made her remember why that teenage crush was still important.

Because it wasn't just something that had happened ten years ago. It was something that had started that day, and had haunted her in one way or another ever since.

She'd thought she'd escaped the feeling of not being good enough when she was in California, with a new husband and a successful career. And then that had crashed, and she'd come back home and she'd seen Jack Taylor when she'd been at her most desperate and vulnerable, and it was as if those ten years had never happened.

The seventeen-year-old Kitty, clutching two paper cups of punch, had stood on the gym dance floor in her silly high heels and gawped at the sight of the boy she loved kissing Melissa Beauchamp. She had heard someone giggle, laughing at her. Kitty had blinked and seen the entire order of her life rearrange itself.

She wasn't good enough. She'd tried for the one thing, the one person she'd wanted most in the world, and he'd humiliated her in front of the entire school. She'd had a dream, and it had exploded.

And that one moment, that one disappointment, had set a pattern for the rest of her life.

Thus, the Kitty Giroux luck had been born.

But she wasn't going to admit that to Jack, even though

when she'd started telling her story she'd wanted him to understand every bit of it. He was sitting on the bench in front of her now, a charming half-smile on his face, a charmingly quizzical expression in his eyes, and she knew exactly how he'd react to her admission.

He'd laugh. And that would be the final straw.

"No," she said. "It's not extreme. Because you haven't changed at all since then."

Jack stood. He walked over to her and put his hands on her shoulders. Kitty felt the warmth from him against the whole of her body; she felt his strength and his breadth and tallness surrounding her, even out here in the cool air, in plain sight of all the neighbors.

My God, she wanted him. Even though she was angry with him. Even though she didn't trust him.

Maybe even more, because she was angry and mistrustful. Because she could never have him.

"Look at me, Kitty," he said, and the rough intimacy of his voice made her shiver. He lifted her chin with one hand. He wasn't smiling anymore. "You can't say I haven't changed. I have. And you have, too. We're both adults now."

Adult was right. As in adjective, meaning sexually charged. As in *adult movie.*

Jack's other hand slid down to her hip, and he pulled her closer to him. Close enough so that her breasts, in their flimsy top, brushed his chest. He looked down and tightened his hand on her. She knew he could see, even through her bra, how her nipples had involuntarily hardened.

"We're not kids anymore," he said. His chest vibrated against her exquisitely sensitive breasts. "We can act on what we feel. And nobody has to get hurt." Slowly, he dipped his head toward hers, tilted his mouth, a breath away from her lips.

Even before he could kiss her, she knew all the glory of it. She knew her body had come alive as soon as she'd seen him.

She knew her arms were curling themselves around him, and that she was leaning into him, wanting him all around her, inside her, now.

Her subconscious saved her.

It brought her the memory of her senior photograph in her high-school yearbook. The determined set of her chin as she showed the world that she was going to succeed at everything she tried. And her senior ambition: "To be the best."

She'd been wrong. She'd been foolish, and naïve and unlucky. But now she needed that ambition to be true. For once, at last, after all the disappointments in her life—her father, her divorce, her career—she needed to be first. The best. That was why she'd come to Maine to make a new start.

And she'd never be first with Jack. She couldn't be the best. She'd only ever be the latest.

"Jack. Stop."

He stopped. She felt his breath feather against her lips, his muscles trembling with sudden restraint. She stepped back, even though the separation hurt.

"Your body might have grown up," she said. Her voice sounded very loud in her own ears. "But you haven't. You're still out for one thing. And me and Melissa Beauchamp have one thing in common. I'm not going to have sex with you, either."

CHAPTER SEVEN

"SO YOU'RE going to Providence for the weekend after all?" Sue asked that evening.

Kitty put her suitcase down on the kitchen floor. "Yeah. You're right, I need to have some fun, and Marie's parties are always fun. Knowing her, she'll have invited loads of single guys."

"What about Jack Taylor?"

"I'm not interested in Jack Taylor, Mom. He's got plenty of girlfriends already, he doesn't need me. Besides, I promised Marie on the phone this morning that I'd come down for her party."

What a lie. Kitty hadn't talked to Marie for weeks. She was leaving town for one reason and one reason only: Jack.

The thought of maybe running into him by mistake, or him turning up unannounced at her mother's house again, sent her palms sweating and her thoughts running for cover. She wanted to be miles away from him. At the same time, she couldn't be close enough to him. Just being in the same city with him was fraying her nerves to the breaking point.

Quite simply, Portland wasn't big enough for the both of them.

Sue Giroux put the kettle on the stove, and then came over to Kitty to smooth her hair back behind her ears. She waited until her mother turned to take down the tea canister, and pulled her hair loose again.

"Well, I'm glad you stayed for the barbecue, anyway," her mother said. "It was good to have the family together this afternoon for once." She sighed. "It hardly happens anymore, with you and Nick busy all the time."

Kitty felt instantly guilty for her lie and her small hair-related act of rebellion. She pushed the tendrils back behind her ears and gave her mother a big hug and kiss before she picked up her bag and went out the door.

She climbed into her convertible with a distinct feeling of escape. Her heart lifted as soon as she turned the key in the ignition and started down the road. Providence was three hours' drive away, far enough from Jack. And Marie was just the person she needed to see. Marie knew Jack Taylor nearly as well as she did; she'd been Kitty's best friend in high school, after all. Marie would make her laugh about the whole situation. She'd give Kitty a sense of perspective and make her realize that there were plenty of other men in existence besides charming, heartless Jack.

And then after the long weekend, her confidence restored, feeling like a grown-up rather than a gawky, horny teenager, Kitty could face Jack Taylor again and get back to work on the Delphi.

She'd stop on the way in Portsmouth, she decided. She'd pick up the most expensive bottle of wine she could afford at the New Hampshire state liquor store. It wouldn't be fancy, but she and Marie could drink it together and reminisce about the good and bad old days.

She won't believe how gorgeous he's turned out, Kitty thought. *And how amazing the Delphi is.* She could show Marie the pictures she'd taken on her digital camera. And her drawings. In fact, she needed to do some more drawings this weekend, so she could show them to Dave, the foreman, on Tuesday.

Kitty braked and signalled right to turn down a side street

and back to her mother's house. She'd forgotten to pack the camera. Odd, she hadn't seen it today, or she would've taken some pictures at the barbecue.

Then she hit the brakes again, far more sharply than necessary for stopping at the next intersection.

She hadn't seen the camera today because she'd left it at the cinema. Along with her sketch pad, her pencils, and her floorplans of the Delphi. Everything she needed for work.

"Drat!" A car pulled up behind her, so Kitty had no choice but to accelerate.

Well, she'd just have to do without the camera for the rest of the weekend. And her work. It would be letting Dave down, but—

No. Jack had made her act like a stupid kid far too many times already. If she wanted her camera and her sketch pad, she'd go get them, and she'd behave like a normal adult human being while she did. And then she'd drive to Providence to see Marie, and she'd get *two* bottles of wine on the way, and she'd make Marie take her to a trendy bar somewhere and she'd flirt with all the single guys she saw.

She tightened her grip on the wheel and drove toward the Delphi.

The big outside door creaked open without her having to use her key, and Kitty felt her stomach leap in dismay—or was it excitement?—realizing Jack was probably in the building somewhere.

It didn't matter. If she was lucky, Jack would be up in his office, and she wouldn't have to see him. She practically tiptoed into the building, pulling the outer door and then the inner door to the vestibule shut behind her.

Popcorn. The smell of it filled the whole high-ceilinged lobby, instantly evocative of Friday-night double features and Saturday-afternoon matinees. For the first time, the vast, empty space around her really felt like what it was: a movie theater.

She looked at the concession stand. A gleaming steel machine stood behind the counter. Yellow light poured from its glass case, which was lined at the bottom with a fluffy cloud of popcorn. Jack's bicycle leaned against the wall next to the stand. But there was no other sign of him.

Softly, making no sound in her sneakers, Kitty headed toward the closed double doors at the end of the lobby. As usual, she skirted the trapdoor in the floor. Even though it had been repaired, she still didn't trust it. It would be just her luck to fall through it as Jack had.

The only noise was the muffled explosion of corn kernels in the popper. A few more steps and she'd be through the light trap, in the cinema, and she could grab her camera and get the hell out of the state for the rest of the weekend.

"Katherine." Jack's voice made her jump. She turned and saw his head peering over the counter of the concession stand. As she watched he stood and dusted off his jeans. "You want some popcorn?"

I am a normal adult human being, and I will act that way. "No, thank you."

Stop looking at his mouth.

"Come to apologize for kicking me out of your family barbecue this afternoon? Or do you want to reconsider whether you'll have sex with me?"

Kitty clenched her teeth. "I left my camera here yesterday." She strode forward through the wooden doors, through the light trap, down the aisle of the theater to where her camera still perched on the end of a seat next to her portfolio. She swiped them up and walked determinedly back up the sloped aisle, past where Jack still stood watching her, to the closed door to the vestibule.

She felt his eyes on her the entire time—those brown eyes that had burned into her after he kissed her, his pupils dilated with desire. Kitty reached out with sweaty hands for the door and twisted and pulled.

The handle came off.

Kitty looked down at the tarnished brass knob in her hand. Then she looked at the thick wooden door, her escape route to Providence and Marie. The thick wooden *closed* door. She shut her eyes in pure horror.

The Kitty Giroux bad luck. It never failed.

No. This could not be as bad as it looked. It was probably just loose, and she could put it back. Kitty opened her eyes and lifted the handle to the hole where it used to be. There was a little bit of metal protruding from the handle that should fit into the hole. For a joyous moment she felt it slide into place, but then she tried to turn it and it fell heavily into her hand again.

"Damn." She knelt down and peered at the hole and the handle end more closely. It looked as if the handle had actually broken off, leaving part of itself in the hole.

She tried it again anyway. No luck.

As usual.

Kitty sank to the floor. She put her head in her hands and moaned into her palms.

"What's going on?" Jack had come up behind her.

Kitty held the door handle up to him. "Your stupid building broke."

"What?" He took the handle from her and tried to fit it back into place.

"I've tried that. It doesn't work. It's snapped off."

Of course, he had to try it for himself before he'd believe her. Typical male.

"It's broken," he said as if he were discovering some incredible new fact.

"That's what I said. Weren't you listening?"

"What did you do to it?"

Kitty scrambled to her feet. "I didn't do anything to it. I just turned it."

"You must have turned it pretty hard. This metal is about half an inch thick."

"What do I look like, an Amazon? I turned it like a normal door handle. It's not my fault this place is a scrap heap."

"You must have jerked it or something."

Jerk was right. "I didn't."

"This door isn't even normally closed," he said. "You've been working here for nearly two months now, you must've noticed that it's never closed. Why did you close it in the first place?"

That was it. Kitty lost her temper. "Because I wasn't thinking! Because I was a bundle of nerves coming in here! Because all of my worst suspicions were confirmed the minute I walked in and you made that stupid jerkface comment about having sex! I just closed it, okay? I didn't know I was going to get dissected alive for doing it!"

The last of her words echoed away and the Delphi suddenly felt very, very quiet. She was standing less than a foot from Jack, glaring into eyes that blazed into hers with equal intensity. The burst of hot temper she had felt a moment ago turned into something deeper, warmer, something that made her cheeks flush and her breasts feel heavy. Her tongue remembered the taste of him, and her lips parted themselves.

Jack's eyes left hers and dipped downward for a split second to look at her. He didn't step closer, but Kitty felt as if he had taken her in his arms again. That same exhilaration, the mad wanting, the spinning around into something dizzyingly dangerous.

Her lips tingled. Her fingers tingled. Her whole body tingled, and she didn't want it to tingle. She wanted to go to Providence.

She dragged in a breath and stepped back before he looked back up into her eyes. "Listen. It's no big deal," she said. "I'm sure you can get it fixed." Another step back. "Anyway. I'll just leave by the fire exit."

"They're locked." His voice was quiet. "I don't have the key."

Incredulity and desperation wrestled for the top position in her emotions. Incredulity won. "You don't have your key with you?"

"No. I came right here after I left you, to set up the popcorn machine. I didn't bring all my keys with me, just the front door one that's on my normal key chain."

Desperation picked itself up off the floor and squared off with incredulity again. "Isn't it totally illegal not to have fire escapes open?"

"Probably. But the place isn't exactly open to the public yet." Jack pushed on the door. It didn't budge.

"The place isn't exactly open at *all*. Jack, what were you thinking?"

"I'm not the one who closed the only exit and then wrenched the handle off the door."

She chose to ignore his accusatory tone this time. "Okay. I know there are no windows down here, but what about the skylights upstairs?"

"They've got bars over them." He braced his shoulder against the door and pushed again. The muscles in his thighs bunched against his jeans and the cords of his neck stood out with the effort. The door stayed shut.

"Is there a big ventilation duct or something we can get through?" She knew there wasn't—she'd been over the blueprints of this place with a fine-tooth comb—but she asked anyway, as if saying it would make the duct exist.

Jack shook his head. He pushed again, his breath whooshing out as he forced his body against the unmoving door.

Desperation got incredulity in a headlock and threw it clear out of the ring. "Then how are we going to get out of here?" she asked.

He stopped pushing and leaned sideways on the door. "It might help if you pushed, too."

"Oh. Yeah. Okay." She planted her palms next to Jack's shoulder on the door.

"On three. One. Two. Three."

She shut her eyes and pushed as hard as she could, and felt Jack beside her tall and strong, heard his breath hiss out between clenched teeth. *Please move, door,* she pleaded silently. *Please move.* Her muscles protested and began to tremble.

But the door stayed shut.

Jack's outrush of breath, a sudden small relaxing of the tension in the air, told her he'd stopped pushing. She opened her eyes and sagged against the stubborn door.

"Please tell me the phone lines were installed ahead of schedule," she gasped.

"They're going in next Thursday." Jack chewed on his lip and narrowed his eyes at the door. "The hinges for this door are on the other side, or I'd try to take them off. Let's push again, let's really give it a bang this time. Come here."

Kitty joined him about a yard from the door. "Don't you have a cell phone?"

"Haven't been able to find it. Probably somewhere in my house. Okay, think of the thing you hate most in the world and throw yourself against the door like you're trying to knock it into next week. Ready? On three."

Kitty thought of the sleek silver splinters of her phone lying in the car dealer's lot, two months ago. She clenched her fists and at Jack's "three" she hurled her body forward. Her shoulder and hip crashed into the door. She heard the thud as Jack hit at the same time as her. But the door didn't even tremble.

They both retreated, rubbing their shoulders. Kitty's arms ached and her shoulder throbbed. She sat on the floor, leaning against the wall.

Jack sat cross-legged facing her. "One good thing is that the outside door is still unlocked. And the handle on the other side of this inner door might still work. So all we have to do is wait for someone to come along and open it."

Kitty brightened. "That's not too bad. You must have some

workmen or something scheduled to come by this weekend, right?"

"No. It's Memorial Day weekend, remember? They're not coming till Tuesday. I wasn't planning on being here myself, but the popcorn machine got delivered and I wanted to see if it worked. And then I got kicked out of your barbecue."

"But people know you're here, right? They'll get worried when you don't show up for something and they'll come here to find you." Her voice sounded a little too high-pitched. She swallowed and tasted dust.

"No. I didn't have any plans for the weekend. Nobody's expecting me anywhere. I rode my bike straight from your house, to here. By the way, I hope you apologized to your mother for my having to leave so quickly after she'd invited me. I didn't get a chance to, with you ordering me off the premises."

"She'll deal with it," Kitty said.

"That does put my mind at rest. Does your family know you've come here?"

"No. I was going to Providence to see my friend Marie until Monday night."

"Does she have your mother's number? Will she call her when you don't turn up?"

Kitty bit her lip. "Marie doesn't know I'm coming. She invited me three weeks ago and I said no at first, but then I decided this evening I'd go."

"After you had that argument with me? Couldn't stand to be in the same city?"

"Exactly."

"Great. Thanks. Well, you're stuck with me now." Jack checked his watch. "It's seven-thirty on Saturday evening, and we're trapped in this building, and nobody expects to see either one of us until Monday night."

Desperation rose in her throat again. "There must be someone else who might come by to do something? What about Oz?"

"Oz flew to Montreal last night for the weekend. He's speaking at some psychology conference there." Jack ran his hand through his hair, leaving finger trails in its dark thickness. "Nobody is going to come here. We're stuck."

Kitty launched herself to her feet and pounded her fists against the door. "Help!" she yelled at the top of her voice. "Somebody please help!"

She pounded and pounded and pounded until her fists felt bruised and her voice cracked. Then she slid limply to the floor.

"Is it really that bad to be locked in here with me?" Jack asked her.

Kitty looked at him. His black hair rumpled, his jeans molded to his muscular legs.

God, it was the best thing in the world. And her worst nightmare, at the same time.

"I can think of better ways to spend a weekend," she said.

He glared at her. "You really know how to make a guy feel good, you know that?"

"Somehow making you feel good isn't exactly my priority right now."

"That's funny. Making you feel good has been my priority for weeks."

"Would you stop it with the suggestive remarks!"

Jack's mouth dropped open. Then he closed it. "Actually," he said slowly, "that wasn't meant as a suggestive remark. I have been trying to make you feel good. I've been trying to be your friend."

"Oh."

She must've looked as surprised as she felt, because the anger in Jack's eyes melted away and she saw them crinkle a bit in the corners. "Geez," he said, "and you accuse *me* of reducing everything to sex."

His teasing upper lip, tightening in a suppressed smile. The sudden sparkle in his brown eyes.

How on earth was she supposed to not think of sex?

"Well," she said briskly, "if you want to make me feel good, get that door open. I'll go look at the skylights upstairs."

The skylights upstairs were barred with iron as immovable as the door downstairs, but checking them gave Kitty a few minutes' breathing space, at least. When she came back down to the lobby, Jack was kneeling in front of the door, inserting a credit card into the tiny gap between the door and the jamb.

"I don't understand," he said. "This always works in the movies." He wiggled the card, and a small snap reached Kitty's ears. "Damn. There goes another perfectly good platinum card."

Kitty sucked on her bruised fist and kicked a cardboard box. "Speaking of movies, please tell me that the film projector is working and we can at least watch something while we're waiting to be rescued." Her throat hurt from yelling.

"Nope. The light works, but the reels don't turn. New one won't be delivered till August. You got a credit card I can use?"

"I don't have any credit cards." She wandered over to the concession stand, where the popcorn machine still popped away happily, as if nothing were wrong. "My God, what have you got back here?"

She picked up a yellow box from the huge stack behind the counter. "Raisinets," she read.

"Yeah, I ordered them with the popcorn; it all got delivered this morning. We won't starve, at least."

Kitty replaced the box and walked over to where Jack knelt. "Jack. You mean to tell me that we're stuck inside a cinema with the strongest door in the world. There are no windows. You don't have a telephone. The fire exit's locked shut. There isn't even a working film projector. But you have a popcorn machine and a year's supply of chocolate-covered raisins?"

Jack's mouth twitched ever so slightly.

"What? What other totally useless thing do you have in here?"

The twitch turned into half a smile. "About a gross of condoms."

Kitty threw her hands up in the air. "Great. One hundred and forty-four of them? So if we get bored, we can fill them with water and have a fight."

He raised one eyebrow. "There are other possible uses for them, you know."

"Yeah, like if you don't stop making suggestive remarks I can stretch one over your head to shut you up."

Jack threw back his head and laughed. And laughed. He clapped his hands to his stomach and fell back on the floor, gasping for air.

Kitty couldn't help it. She laughed, too. First, at the mental picture of Jack with a condom stretched over his head. Then at the sight of him lying on the ground, a grown, gorgeous man helpless with laughter.

He looked up at her, grinning. His cheeks were flushed and his eyes bright and sparkling. "Point taken. Remark withdrawn." He wiped his eyes. "I'm sorry I blamed you for breaking the door. It wasn't your fault."

All the tension and frustration seemed to have left her with her laughter. "It's okay. I'm sorry I called your theater stupid."

"And I'm sorry I broke your heart in high school."

With Jack's remark, all the breath left her body, too. Kitty sat down with a bump on the parquet floor across from him.

She'd thought she hadn't wanted an apology from Jack. But now that she had it, she knew how much she'd wanted it.

"What brought that on?" she gasped.

"Because I am sorry. It was a bad thing to do. And I shouldn't have gotten defensive about it this afternoon. But it's hard to be attacked for something you did ten years ago, Kitty. It's the present that matters to me, not the past. But the past seems to keep on preventing us from having any sort of a relationship."

"It's not the past that's preventing us," Kitty said. Her voice was hoarse. "It's the fact that, to you, the word 'relationship' is synonymous with 'recreational sex'."

"You're saying this because I've slept with a few women."

"More than a few, I'd guess."

"Okay. More than a few. I don't understand your problem with that, though. I've already said that the other women don't matter to me. It's you that I want."

His saying it so boldly made her shiver. Kitty pressed her palms hard against the floor to keep her anchored in one place. "You don't get it at all, Jack. That's exactly why I don't trust you."

"Because I want you?"

How did he do that? Make this huge room seem suddenly far, far too small? "No. Because the women in your past don't matter to you. You've been intimate with them. You've shared something incredibly important with them. But they're not important to you. They're bodies. Not people with feelings."

Jack stood up and brushed off his jeans. "Kitty, I can see how you'd reach that conclusion. But it's just not true. I've been friends with every single woman I've slept with."

"Friends? Never anything more?"

"What's wrong with being friends?" He came over and sat down next to her. He took her hand in his and even that small contact sent a rush of awareness through Kitty. His hand was warm and surrounded hers completely.

"Look," he said. "I think I know what you're getting at. You think I've left a string of broken hearts behind me. But I haven't. I don't hurt women. If they get involved with me, they know the score. I'm not interested in settling down. I'm out for a good time, and so are the women I get involved with."

"So they know the rules." She tried, on principle, to pull her hand away, but he didn't let her.

"It's not rules, it's reality."

"And you've never hurt a woman who expected more."

He exhaled slowly. "Not since you."

"How do you know?"

Jack stood and pulled her to her feet. "I think we need popcorn to have this conversation. Do you want some?"

With the word "popcorn", Kitty's stomach suddenly growled. She hadn't eaten much at the barbecue after Jack had turned up, and it was way past supper time. "Is there butter?"

Jack let go of her hand, swung himself over the concession stand counter and picked up two cardboard tubs from beside the machine. "Large buttered popcorn coming up." He scooped the containers full of popcorn, drizzled hot liquid topping on them, and handed one over to her. "Come on. Let's go sit in the cinema. The seats are more comfortable than the floor in here."

"Why do I get the feeling that I'm not going to like what you tell me?" Kitty asked, following him through the light trap into the auditorium.

"Probably because you won't. But talking with you today made me think about what really happened that night at the prom. And I think I owe you the truth. Have a seat."

The chairs hadn't been reupholstered yet—they were waiting until the painting was done—but a few of them in front were covered with a relatively clean dust sheet. Kitty sat on one of them, and Jack sat beside her. She ate a piece of popcorn without tasting it.

"I didn't want to make out with Melissa Beauchamp at the prom," Jack said. "I did it on the spur of the moment, because she was there. And I did it because I wanted you to see me kissing her."

"Why?" she whispered.

She knew why. She wasn't pretty enough. She didn't wear the right clothes. She wasn't funny enough or talented enough. She wasn't the *best.*

"You cared too much," Jack said, and sighed. "I hadn't realized it before we went to the prom. You always acted friendly, you never told me you'd had this big crush. But the minute I kissed you I could tell. It all meant something to you. It mattered. You had all of this emotion."

He frowned and rubbed his forehead. "I liked you, Kitty; I liked you a lot. You were pretty and we had a great time together. But when I kissed you I suddenly felt…responsible for your happiness. And that was too much. So I freaked out, I guess." He shrugged. "I wasn't grown up enough to tell you that I couldn't deal with how you felt about me. So I acted like a typical teenage boy and did the easy, cruel thing instead of the hard, kind thing."

Kitty put her tub of popcorn down on the floor. If she ate it now, she'd choke.

"I was just a kid, but it was still wrong," he said. "It was the wrong way to tell you I couldn't handle a relationship. So that's why I owe you an apology."

He'd seen even then that she was desperate. He'd known how much she wanted him. She'd always thought he had, but now she knew.

She couldn't say anything.

Jack stood. "It was nothing against you, Kitty. I couldn't handle what you wanted. I knew I'd hurt you, and that made me feel bad. So from then on, I tried to make sure that nothing like that would happen again."

He punctuated his words with hand gestures. "I learned from it. That prom night changed me. I started telling the women I dated that I didn't want to get emotionally involved, right up front, so that misunderstandings like ours didn't happen. I don't hurt women, Kitty. I'm honest about the extent of my relationships before we begin, and all the way through. And it doesn't happen often, but if I feel like a woman is getting too attached to me, I end it. By talking with her. And we stay friends."

"So it's because of me that you've become such a wonderful communicator and therefore get to have as much no-strings-attached sex as you want," Kitty said, quietly. Bitterly.

"No, it's not because of you. It's because of me. Because of who I am, and what I want. And I'll apologize for treating you badly in high school, but I won't apologize for who I am."

He was pacing now, his arms crossed in front of his chest. "To my thinking, I'm being more honest than if I stuck with a relationship that I didn't really want because I didn't want to let somebody down. Or if I fooled myself that I was in love when all I felt was friendship. At least I haven't ended up a few years down the line with a messy divorce."

Kitty stood, too. "Like what happened with me and my ex-husband, you mean? Yes, I see how your way is much better. Thanks for explaining it to me."

She turned and began to walk up the aisle of the cinema, not knowing where she was going. Not caring. She'd walk straight through the broken door if she had to. Anything to get away from Jack Taylor and his honesty.

"Kitty!"

Jack ran past her and stood in front of the door, blocking her way. She stopped, her fists clenched and her chest heaving. She was angry, but she was turned on by him, too, and that made her even angrier.

"What would you know about divorce, Jack? What makes you such an expert on relationships? You've never had one! You've never been in love. You've never cared about anybody except for yourself. You've never had anybody leave you, you've never lost somebody. So forgive me if I don't feel like listening to your great theories about the joys of communication."

He held up his hands. "Okay. All right. I put my foot in my mouth. It was a thoughtless remark, and I'm sorry I made it." He took a step toward her. "And you're right that I've never had somebody leave me. But it's not fair to take it all out on me. I was a jerk when I was eighteen. But whatever else has happened to you isn't my fault."

There was a pause, while both of them stared at each other.

Jack, still and serious; Kitty, tense and full of fury. Then Kitty hitched in a deep breath, and let it out slowly.

"No. It's not your fault. None of it is your fault, really. Except that you can't be the person I want you to be. And that's not your fault, either."

His brow furrowed. "What kind of person do you want me to be?"

Kitty shook her head. She felt very tired, all of a sudden. "Nobody. Don't worry about it, Jack. Can we stop fighting now for a little while?"

"I'd like to stop fighting." He put one hand on her shoulder, and with the other he stroked her hair back from her face. Like holding her hand, it was a tender gesture. He brushed his fingers over her cheekbone and down the side of her face.

She should move away. But it felt so, so wonderful.

"Tell me, Kitty," he said. "What kind of a person do you want me to be? I've been trying to figure it out." He cupped her face in his palm. His brown eyes made her feel as if she were melting into a pool of chocolate.

"I want you to—" *Be the person I've always dreamed about. Jack Taylor, in love with me.* She swallowed. She couldn't say that. "It doesn't matter."

"I think it does." He tilted up her chin and kissed her forehead, and then her cheek. Each kiss left a little warmth, a little moisture, on her skin. "It's just the two of us in here," he murmured. "Tell me what you want."

"I want—"

Another light kiss on her nose, then on her right eyebrow. The hand that had been on her shoulder held the other side of her face. "What do you want, Kitty?"

"I want you," she whispered.

He kissed her mouth. His lips were warm and gentle. They lingered on hers, drew back, then pressed harder. She opened her mouth to him, just a little, and let her tongue touch his.

Like electricity. Threatening to destroy all her defenses, to reduce her to nothing more than sensation. She lifted her palm to his face and felt the beginnings of beard stubble on his cheek. After three nights, it would be almost long enough to be soft.

Three nights together with Jack. She would be naked, open to him. How would she protect herself?

She pulled back an inch from his face. "Jack," she breathed. "I can't."

He stopped. He looked at her, into her eyes.

"I want to, but I can't," she said. "Please don't make me do something I'll regret. I'm stuck here with you, and if you keep on touching me I'll have sex with you, and I shouldn't do that."

She was close enough to see his lips were moist from her mouth. "What do you want me to do?" he asked.

"Stop touching me. Please. Don't touch me anymore. I'm—" She swallowed, hard. "I need you to stop, because I'm not sure if I can."

As if to prove it, her hand swept down his neck to his chest in a wild, involuntary caress.

She saw Jack swallow, too. "Are you sure?"

Not at all. But it was the safest option. "Yes," she said.

He dropped his hands from her face and stepped back from her.

Kitty blinked. She hadn't actually expected him to do what she asked.

Maybe that was even why she'd asked him in the first place.

"Thank you," she said. It was for the best. She stepped back and leaned against the back row of seats.

Jack looked as if he were in pain. "You're welcome," he said. He ran both of his hands through his hair, leaving grooves in its glossiness. "That wasn't easy."

"No. But thank you."

They stood there, staring at each other. The air was thick.

"What should we do?" Jack asked.

Kitty opened her mouth, and then shut it. She checked her

watch. "It's still early, but maybe we should get some sleep and try to get rescued again in the morning."

"All right."

She looked around the cinema. "Where's the best place to sleep, do you think?" She was going to be sleeping in the same room as Jack.

"Well, the lobby is closer to the restrooms and the entrance, but it's carpeted in here. Let's go down in front of the stage, where it's flat."

She kept a careful distance from him as they walked down the aisle.

Jack jumped onto the stage and opened one of the huge cardboard boxes that sat on the side. He pulled out handfuls of vivid crimson material. "Look. The perfect blankets."

"Those are the new curtains for the stage. We can't use those, we'll crush the velvet."

He kept on pulling swathes of fabric out. "It's okay. I'll have them cleaned afterwards. One should be enough for both of us; they're big enough that we'll each have plenty of space."

Sharing a velvet curtain with the sexiest man in the universe? Kitty watched him doubtfully. "That'll be a huge cleaning bill, Jack."

"If I had my choice, Kitty, we'd be sharing a suite in the most exclusive coastal resort I could find. The cleaning bill will be peanuts compared to that. Besides, do you really want to sleep on a paint-spattered dust sheet?"

"There's some sort of logic there," she agreed, and helped him take the massive curtain out of the box. The velvet was deep and rich and soft, exactly what she'd chosen for a rather different purpose than sleeping on. When it was spread out on the floor, it took up nearly the entire space in front of the row of seats.

"I'll take this side, and you can have that one," Jack said, pointing. "We can roll ourselves up in the velvet."

"All right. I'll, um, use the ladies' room first."

Jack walked with her up the aisle back into the lobby. She went into the ladies' room, and he went into the men's. Kitty washed as much dust as she could from her hands and face, and brushed her teeth with her finger and water. When she came out of her restroom, Jack was just coming out of his. They walked back into the cinema and down the aisle together, side by side.

We're going to bed together, Kitty thought again.

"Have this." He was wearing a light gray zip-up sweatshirt, and he took it off and held it out toward Kitty. "You're only wearing a little T-shirt, you might get cold."

"No, that's okay. You keep it."

"No. I insist. The heating isn't hooked up, and it gets cold at night in May."

Kitty took it. Sure enough, it smelled like Jack. Not only was she going to be sleeping in the same building with him wrapped up in the same length of material, but every breath she took would have him in it.

Who was she kidding? Every breath she'd taken since she'd first set foot in the Delphi had had Jack Taylor in it.

Kitty put on the sweatshirt and took off her shoes and lay down on the velvet curtain. She pulled a length of it over her curled up into its softness and closed her eyes. She could hear Jack moving: slipping off his sneakers, unzipping his jeans and pulling them off. He was going to sleep in his T-shirt and underwear next to her, in this curtain.

"I thought you said it was going to be cold. Why are you taking off your jeans?" she managed to ask.

"I'd rather be cold than have rivets digging into my hips all night," he said. She heard him walking barefoot up the aisle toward the light switches.

She kept her eyes screwed shut tight and wondered if Jack wore boxers or briefs. Then she tried to banish from her head the image of him wearing either style of underwear.

It didn't work. Surrounded by Jack, enveloped in Jack, her thoughts full of Jack, Kitty curled deeper into the red velvet and waited for him to turn out the lights and join her.

Jack stared up into the darkness, every muscle tensed.

A crush.

That was what it was. At age twenty-eight, he had a massive, planet-size crush on Katherine Giroux Clifford.

He'd made the connection this afternoon, sitting on that bench. As soon as she had described how he had laughed and what he had had for lunch one day in his sophomore year of high school, something had clicked in his mind.

Here was the explanation of why he had been completely crazy since hearing her voice. Why he remembered every single movement of her body since then, every word she said, every heart-stopping moment when she smiled. Why now, despite the darkness and the space between them, he could imagine her body tucked inside the curtain, inside his sweatshirt, her breasts rising and falling against this material that he had touched. Her hair spread out on the velvet. Her delicate eyelids closed over those incredible green eyes.

He heard and felt her shifting inside the curtain. She would be so warm, so soft. Jack wrapped himself tighter in the material and tried to control his breathing.

He had a crush. That was all. And a crush was nothing to get worked up over. Even if he'd never had one before, there was no way he was going to let a crush rule his life. He knew now how Kitty must have felt in high school, how desperate she must have been. And that was why, of course, he felt so bad about what he'd put her through, even now, ten years later. That was the explanation—he could sympathize with her, because for the first time he was going through it himself. That had to be the reason why he felt as if everything she said was vital. As if everything that hurt her hurt him, too; made him feel he had to justify and explain himself in a way he'd never felt he had to do before.

She moved again and let out a small sigh. His mind immediately filled with the image of her mouth, soft, pink and parted, as sweet as he'd dreamed it would be.

"Kitty, are you asleep?" he whispered.

"No."

"Were you really in love with your husband? Or was it more like a crush?"

He felt and heard her turn over. "Why are you asking me this?"

"Like you said. I don't really know what relationships are like. I was wondering."

She sighed. "I cared a lot about Sam. I thought he adored me. He said he did. He seemed safe. And a good man. I thought we could make it work."

"But it didn't."

"He'd had a tempestuous relationship with his first wife. And in the end, he decided to go back to her. To go for passion, instead of safety."

"So he was someone else who left you."

"Yes, Jack."

It bothered him. Why did it bother him? Because Sam had hurt her? Because he, himself, had hurt her?

Yes. But it was also because, for the first time, he could imagine how it might feel to be left.

That was why he'd run up the aisle after her. Even though rationally, he knew there was no way that Kitty could get through that locked door. He couldn't bear for her to leave him.

She spoke again. "But I thought you said the past didn't matter."

"It doesn't." Of course not. The past had never bothered him before.

It was because he had a crush, and crushes made you act weird. Look at Kitty—she'd had a crush on him for three years in high school, and never said anything about it. Now that was weird. Sweet, but weird.

That had to be the reason why, against all reason and desire, he'd stopped touching her when she'd said that if he kept on, she'd have sex with him. He could be having sex with her now, if he hadn't stopped. She wanted to. He wanted to. But suddenly her needs seemed more important than their wants.

Crushes made you act…stupid.

Still, it was good news that what he'd been going through was nothing serious, just a crush. He could stop worrying now. Probably if he stopped worrying about it, it would lessen, and he could start feeling more like himself again.

Jack closed his eyes. Now that he knew why he was so obsessed with Kitty, maybe he could even get some sleep.

"I'm going to sleep now, Jack," she whispered. "Goodnight."

"Me, too. Goodnight," he whispered back. Though even as he said it he knew he was wrong.

There was no way in hell he was going to sleep.

CHAPTER EIGHT

HE WAS LYING beside her and they weren't in the Delphi. They were in a bed. Her hair lay vibrant on the white pillow.

He could smell her. Warm, a hint of vanilla. Her hand felt like velvet around his erection. This time he wanted her even more.

Kitty guided him to her, and wrapped her leg around his hip. Inch by inch, he sank into her, slowly, feeling how wet and ready she was. A corner of Jack's mind knew he was dreaming this, knew he was really locked in the Delphi and he'd never made love with Kitty. Knew he could smell her scent because she lay close to him on a red velvet curtain in real life.

But as he felt her smile with his fingers, as he tasted her fingertips with his tongue, as he moved deep within her, he knew this dream was real, too.

Jack abandoned himself to feeling. He felt every separate warmth of her body against his, her breasts against his chest, her thigh around his hip, her breath against his face. He looked deep into her green eyes, felt her muscles contracting around him, and waited for her to call out his name.

Kitty awoke to the scent of coffee and the sight of Jack, dressed in a blue T-shirt and white boxer shorts, sitting cross-legged on the velvet curtain a few feet from her and holding a small flashlight and an aluminum insulated mug.

"What time is it?"

At the sound of her voice, Jack looked up and smiled. "About six in the morning. How did you sleep?"

"Not too bad." What a lie. She'd been hyper-aware of Jack all night; the fact that she could feel as well as hear every movement he made didn't help any. She'd had a restless night, uncertain in the dark of the boundaries between sleep and awareness.

She'd awakened from dreams of Jack beside her, inside her, panting into her ear, to hear his real breathing, so close. She'd sucked in air trying to steady herself and tasted and smelled nothing but Jack. She'd been too hot, and had slipped off her jeans and used them as a pillow.

At one point, she'd heard him groaning aloud, and she'd come awake, whispering, "Jack?" He'd answered her with another groan, and then had fallen back into silence as she'd listened, heart pounding.

Then she'd lapsed back into half-sleep, a fantasy of his hands on her, exploring everywhere, rough and soft as velvet.

Her eyes felt prickly now and her muscles ached. And her entire body was a throbbing mass of need. "How did you sleep?" she asked.

"Lousy. I fell asleep once, but my dreams..." Jack seemed to shake himself. "Want some coffee? I have a kettle up in the office, but I've only got one mug, and no milk or sugar."

"That would be great."

"Good." Jack brought the mug and the flashlight over to her. Kitty sat up, the curtain still covering her bare legs. He sat down next to her and propped the flashlight up in the middle, making a circle of light slant across them.

He'd been at least three yards from her all night and she hadn't been able to sleep because he'd been far too close. Now he was less than twelve inches away from her, and Kitty felt such a bizarre sense of coziness and tension that she wasn't sure where to put her hands.

Kitty took the mug from him and drank the hot, strong liquid. Maybe the caffeine would calm her nerves.

"I couldn't sleep because I was thinking of you," Jack said.

She nearly spat out the coffee. Instead, she swallowed, with difficulty. "Really?" she said, unable to say anything sensible whatsoever.

Jack took the mug from her. "Yes. I've been thinking about your mouth." The flashlight cast half his face into brightness and half into shadow, and outlined the contours of his lips.

"I want to kiss you so much that even touching my lips to the same place on the mug that you drank from is something," he said, and turned the mug around in his hands.

In the second before his lips met the rim, she could see the moist outline of her own lips on the metal. And then his mouth closed around the edge where she had touched it, that teasing upper lip dipping inside, and he drank.

It was nearly a kiss. His eyes didn't leave hers the entire time. And when he lowered the mug, he said, "I have never wanted anyone as much as I want you. I've never lain awake all night remembering a kiss and imagining more. I've never been turned on by the sound of a woman breathing. Or needed to taste her so badly that I've made coffee I don't even want just so I can drink out of the same mug."

He passed the cup to her and Kitty held it between her two hands, unable to drink, or think, or do anything but look at him.

His voice was rough with desire and lack of sleep. "It's a crush, or an obsession, or…something. I don't know. I only know I've never felt this way before."

Neither had she. Since the very first moment she had seen Jack again, she had been sexually aware in a way she'd never been in her life. And now, with the hot mug in her hands feeling cool compared with the fire that was burning in her body, she realized why that was.

It wasn't just her old crush on him making her a hormonal

teenager again. It wasn't because Jack was hitting on her as he hit on every woman within a ten-mile radius.

It was because, quite simply, she wanted Jack Taylor more than she had ever wanted anyone. She always had, and the desire had grown even more as she'd spent time with him. And he, with all his women and his expertise, had never wanted anyone as much as he wanted her right now.

Which, in this one way, made her first. The best.

As she'd always wanted to be.

"Never, Jack?" She could barely say it.

"Not ever, outside of dreams."

Forget the past. Forget the future. Right now, she could have what she wanted. All she had to do was risk taking it.

Carefully, every movement deliberate, she put the coffee down on the floor. And then she turned and leaned forward to kiss Jack.

He met her halfway.

Their lips brushed each other. The first touch was shocking, too real; Kitty drew back a whisper to catch her breath and Jack, unmoving, waited for her to return. And then, slowly, she pressed her mouth to his again.

Kissing him was heaven. His lips, his tongue, his teeth, all the things that made up his smile, his voice, the words he said and his ever-changing expression. It was the magic she'd felt ten years before, spinning on the dance floor in the school gym. And the excitement she'd felt ever since he'd hauled himself out of the hole in the floor and come skidding up beside her.

He was letting her take the lead, responding to her but not pushing her further. Kitty kept it slow. She savored the taste of him: coffee and Jack. He sat motionless on the curtain, his body turned toward her but not touching her. The only place they touched was at the mouth. It was teasing, and sweet, and oh, God, so sexy.

Then Kitty moaned, and Jack made an answering sound

deep in his throat, and the kiss became urgent, devouring, as it had been when they'd kissed all those weeks ago. Frantic. Impatient. Carnal. Kitty grasped his head in her hands and pulled him closer. The day's worth of stubble on his cheeks rasped against her palms and chin. She tangled one hand in his thick hair and with the other she grabbed his shoulder, feeling the tenseness of his muscles, the heat of his skin through his shirt.

But Jack only moved his mouth. His hands stayed by his sides.

Kitty wrenched her mouth from his. "Why aren't you touching me?"

Jack's answer was as breathless as her question. "You asked me not to touch you. I'm waiting for permission."

Kitty, her head spinning, her body clamoring for everything Jack, opened her mouth to reply. "You—"

—have permission to touch me. All over. Now. Please.

But she didn't say it. Because his words proved what she'd learned last night: there was honor in Jack. And they made her start thinking again, beyond this moment and Jack's addictive mouth.

It gave her an idea of how she could satisfy her longing for this man and at the same time safeguard her heart and her career.

"Let me touch you," he whispered, and brought his lips close to hers. Just a breath away.

"No."

Jack froze, and withdrew a little bit. His face looked as if he were in pain. "No?"

With her fingers, she smoothed the crease in his forehead.

"No. You can't touch me. I'll make love with you, Jack. But I can't think about the other women you've had. I need it to be about you and me. And that means that I have to be in control."

She had always responded helplessly to Jack, ever since the age of fourteen. Maybe this way, with her in control, it wouldn't be so dangerous. She could keep her sanity.

"So I can't touch you?"

She nodded. "That's rule number one. Keep your hands to yourself, for this first time. Show me you can do what I ask, just because I ask it. Let me be in control of how this happens. Let me set the pace. Will you do that?"

His eyes were wide; Kitty couldn't quite tell if it was surprise or confusion or plain desire. "Okay."

"Are you sure?"

Jack raised one eyebrow. "Kitty, I will do absolutely anything you ask me to as long as it means that I get to see you naked. Is that sure enough for you?"

"Yeah." She brushed her lips against his again, tasted them with her tongue.

"Rule number two is this. Whatever we do in the Delphi doesn't go beyond it. I'll have an affair with you here and now. Once we're rescued, it's over. We go back to our working relationship. And nothing else. Do you agree?"

He frowned. "Are *you* sure?"

"Of course. I made the rule." She ran her hand down his cheek and the side of his neck, and let her fingers slip inside the collar of his T-shirt. She could keep hold of her emotions, here in the Delphi, if she knew it was only for a short time.

Jack didn't move. "It's just that your rule sounds a lot like the sort of rules you accuse me of making."

"You shouldn't have a problem keeping it, then." She reached further under his shirt to feel his collarbone and the hollow of his shoulder.

Jack swallowed. "Okay. Let's get going, though. Because I have a lot of sexual frustration to work out and somebody might walk through that door any minute now."

"God, I hope not."

And then Kitty wrapped her arms around Jack's neck and pulled him toward her and kissed him with all the passion and longing she'd felt since that day in her freshman year when he'd laughed in the lunch line.

She only broke it off when she felt as if she might explode with wanting him. "Where's that gross of condoms?"

"Right. Yeah. Um, follow me." Jack stood, and Kitty scrambled out of the curtain. Then she got a good look at him in the half-light and started to giggle.

"What?" Jack followed her gaze downward to where the front of his boxer shorts tented out, blatantly showing the length of his erection. He shot her a wry, sexy smile. "Like I said. A lot of sexual frustration."

"Good." Kitty trailed her finger down the front of his boxers, following the taut material to its tip. Jack sucked in his breath sharply.

"Let's—" He swallowed and started again. "Let's go get the condoms. Do you have any change?"

It was her turn to stare at him in surprise. "Change?"

"It's a machine in the men's room. It takes quarters. I don't have any."

"Somehow, I never expected my sex life to depend on having quarters." Kitty shook her head, smiling. She picked up the flashlight from the floor and, Jack behind her, she walked up the aisle and back into the lobby, where her handbag lay beside Jack's bike. "So what do we do if I don't have any?"

He didn't answer. Kitty, mid-rummage, looked up, and that was when the overhead lights went on. She blinked, letting her eyes adjust to the light, and then saw him. He was standing by the switch watching her.

"You're so beautiful," he murmured. "I love your hair. And your legs." He took a step closer, and his gaze swept over her from head to toe. She remembered she'd taken off her jeans, and was only wearing his sweatshirt and her tiny T-shirt over her underwear. She'd been too hot to think about her bare legs before.

Kitty knew she didn't look beautiful. She'd washed off her makeup; she knew her freckles were standing out a mile on her face. Her hair had to be everywhere. And she'd only brushed her teeth with her finger.

But she loved the way Jack was looking at her. It was as if he left a trail of heat, made every inch of her thrill into life.

He licked his lips, and she saw him bite the lower one. "Oh, God, Kitty, I want to touch you so much."

I want you to, she thought. But again, she shook her head. For now, his gaze was enough. His appreciation of her. The naked hunger on his face.

And the fact that he, Jack Taylor, was holding back because she asked him to.

She gave him a small, secret smile, and looked in her purse. "Um, Jack? I only have thirty cents in dimes."

"Right. Come on." His voice was decisive as he strode toward her, and with equal excitement and disappointment Kitty realized that he was going to touch her at last, despite his promise. Her knees went weak and she leaned against the wall, waiting for him to claim her.

He didn't. He walked past her and seized the metal D-lock on his bike. "Follow me."

Her mouth was dry with—what? Fear? Anticipation? Arousal? Kitty followed Jack across the wooden floor, both of them barefoot. His boxer shorts exposed the backs of his thighs and calves; their muscles flexed under their dusting of dark hair. She noticed the sinews at the backs of his knees and imagined her mouth there, nipping at the smooth strong skin.

He led her to the men's room and flipped on the light switch. Kitty blinked again; the white tiles reflected the fluorescent light and made it at least twice as bright as the dusky yellow light in the lobby. The floor was cold underneath her feet.

"What are you doing?" she asked.

"I am not going to let a lack of change stop me from having sex with you. Watch out." Jack swung the D-lock above his head.

"Sorry, Oz," he said, and brought the lock down hard on the

white condom machine on the wall. The metal buckled. Jack frowned and, bunching the muscles in his shoulders and chest, swung down hard again.

The dispenser exploded. Colorful, slippery shrink-wrapped packages slithered from their places and showered around their feet. Kitty heard them hit the tiles with whispering plops. One struck her foot and she read the packaging: Piña Colada Flavored.

Speechless, she looked from the condoms at her feet to Jack. A broad grin was spreading across his face. His twinkling eyes met hers.

"So you think we can get through all of these before Monday night?"

Kitty laughed, and bent down to scoop up an armful of the packets. "There are a hundred and forty-four of these. Do you have that much stamina?"

"With you, I might." He filled his hands with condoms and nodded toward the door. "Should we find a more romantic spot?"

Kitty led the way out of the men's room across the lobby and into the cinema. She turned on the lights and as she walked down the aisle she looked at the space around her: the gilded walls, the high star-speckled ceiling, the red velvet chairs. The red curtain where they'd slept in front of the stage, near the silver screen. Knowing that this improvised bed was going to be the place where she would finally make love with Jack Taylor gave the crumpled crimson fabric a sort of glow. She let the condom packets slide out of her arms and fall onto the floor.

"You're the sexiest thing I've ever seen," she heard Jack murmur behind her. "Do you mind if we start right away so I can touch you soon?"

Kitty shook her hair away from her face and turned to Jack. "I'll get started," she said, curling her fingers around the hem of the shirt he wore. "But I think I might take my time. Pray that no one walks in right now, and raise your arms."

"Please, God, don't let anybody walk in right now." He complied.

She pushed his shirt up, letting the heels of her hands drag over his flesh. Slowly. She felt the firmness of his belly, the ridges of his ribs, the crisp hair on his chest, the steady, fast beating of his heart. Then she pulled the shirt over his head and off, and stepped back to look at him.

Beautiful. There was no other word for it. He was like a classical sculpture, all lean muscle and maleness. He brought his hands back down to his sides and she saw the play of pectorals and biceps, how his forearms tapered down to his sinewy wrists and hands, fleshy thumb pads and long fingers.

She raised her hands to him and let them explore his chest.

She'd touched men before. But she'd never touched Jack. The skin on his shoulders was taut against his bones and muscles. The hollow of his throat thrummed with his heartbeat and his rapid breathing. She raked her fingertips through the black hair on his chest and against his hard nipples. And then she ran her palms down over the ripple of his ribs and abdomen and let the pad of her index finger lie in the shallow indent of his navel.

"Sure I can't touch you?" His hands were clenched in fists by his side.

"Uh-huh." She stroked up the sides of his torso, brought her hands round to clasp his face and pulled his head down to hers.

His kiss showed her how desperate he was to touch her. His tongue thrust into her mouth; his teeth pulled at her lower lip.

"Kitty," he whispered into her mouth, "you are driving me crazy."

"That's the idea," she breathed. She stepped back.

The front of Jack's boxer shorts still outlined the hard shape of his arousal. Carefully, delicately, Kitty hooked her fingertips underneath the elastic of his shorts and pulled them outwards, so they didn't catch on the tip of his erection, and then down.

Keeping her eyes trained on his shorts and not his body, she slid his boxers down his legs. The knuckles of her fingers stroked against his thighs and knees, then his calves and ankles as she knelt before him. Her hair brushed against his skin and her body was so sensitized that it was as if she had extra fingers. When she reached his feet Jack stepped out of his shorts.

Only then did Kitty look. She slowly got to her feet and stepped back and took in all of Jack, from the fine bones of his toes to the glossy hair on the top of his head.

Oh, God, he was magnificent. Lean, strong, every muscle precisely cut with the sinewy, streamlined contours of a cyclist. The dark hair on his chest tapered in a line down his flat belly and then flared out again at his crotch. Where his penis jutted out proudly, fully and gloriously aroused, for her.

For her.

And his face was no less aroused. Jack's eyes met hers and burned deep. She could see his lips were moist from her kissing him.

"You've hardly touched me, and I haven't touched you at all, and I'm more turned on than I have ever been outside of dreams."

His voice, nearly a whisper, held wonder. Just exactly as she felt.

"Jack," she murmured.

"Yes?"

"Nothing. Just—Jack."

This was Jack, who she'd yearned for since the ninth grade. The boy she'd daydreamed about in bed, gripping her pillow and wishing as hard as she could. The person she'd written rapturous notes about, elaborately folded and passed across classroom desks to receive Marie's scribbled reply.

The man who desired her so much he'd agreed not to touch her. Standing before her now and waiting for her to come to him.

Suddenly Kitty felt shy.

She wanted this so much, and she had for such a long time. The feeling of trying, working, hoping, wishing, was so familiar. And so often followed by the feeling of disappointment.

She bit her lip and let her hair fall down over her face. For the first time she noticed the chilly air in the vast space of the cinema. She crossed her arms in front of her chest and pressed her pebbled nipples back into her breasts.

"What's wrong?" Jack took a half-step toward her, his hands outreached, and then seemed to remember himself. He lowered his hands and clenched them at his sides again. "Kitty?"

His voice was deep and rich and spoke her name so intimately. The distance between them shrank into nothing, as it always did whenever he spoke.

"Nothing," she said.

Desperate for him to touch her, glad he wouldn't touch her, Kitty shucked off Jack's sweatshirt. Then she reached down and pulled her T-shirt over her head, her bra and panties off, before she had time to think anymore about what it was she feared about being naked in front of Jack.

His fists unclenched. That was the first thing she saw. Then she noticed he didn't seem to be breathing. Then she looked into his eyes and saw stark, dark longing.

She stepped forward, placed her hands on his shoulders and kissed him again. His mouth was so wonderful, hot and wet and delicious. Her nipples brushed against the crisp hair of his chest. His erection poked her near her navel, then pressed heavy heat against her belly.

He used her closeness to allow him to kiss her face in a hot trail to her ear. "Please," he whispered there, "please let me be inside you. You are so beautiful that I can't stand it."

She stayed there for a long moment, savoring his body against her, loving his breath in her ear. She brought her lips to his own ear and breathed into it.

"Lie down."

He caught her lips with his one more time, lingeringly, before he backed away from her and lay down on his back on the curtain, his hands by his sides.

Kitty scootched down and quickly sorted through the condoms littering the floor around her. Glow In The Dark. Ribbed For Her Pleasure. Exotic Fruit Flavored. Finally, she found some plain regular condoms. *Specially Calibrated for High-School Crush Revisited*, she thought, and giggled a little as she ripped open the cellophane wrapper with her teeth and drew a packet out of the box.

"Are you ready?" she asked.

Jack's head was propped up on one of his arms, and his eyes were scanning her crouching body, from her face to her breasts to her waist to her feet. "I've been more than ready since the minute I saw you," he said.

"I know the feeling," she said, and she tore open the condom wrapper.

One knee lifted over his body, the other pulled close to his hip, and she was straddling him. The feeling of his powerful body against her thighs was incredible. She could see his chest rising and falling rapidly. With every breath, his erection twitched slightly, nearer the curls between her legs.

Licking her lips in anticipation, she took told of Jack's penis in her left hand as she stroked on the latex with her right. He felt impossibly hot, silky-skinned and hard, and he let out a long shuddering breath when she touched him.

"Kitty," he breathed, "please."

Still holding him with her left hand, she lifted herself onto her knees and positioned herself over him. Her right hand stroked over his hips, his chest and then his face. She curled her fingers around his cheekbone, against his jaw, let her thumb slip between his lips.

"Now," she said.

And then she shifted her hips so that the tip of him slid into her. Oh. My. God.

Her eyes locked with Jack's, and she could see that he shared these sensations. They were so deep brown, those eyes. And his face was so expressive. Showing everything that she felt.

She slipped slowly down, feeling every inch of him exquisitely filling her. Her hands rested on his chest just below his nipples, right where she could feel his heartbeat thrumming against his ribs. And then she was there, he was wholly inside her, and she stopped.

"You feel incredible," he said. The corner of his mouth curled up into one of his sexy smiles.

She couldn't help but return it. So, smiling, she leaned down to kiss him, and at the same time she withdrew from him, let him slide out of her until only the tip of him was in her again. And then she shifted her weight back, thrusting him back into her, making them both gasp. She tried it again, slowly up and down, drawing out the sensations.

"This—" he gasped as she slid up on him.

"Is so—" and she slipped back downward.

"Amazing." She reached the bottom, rotated her hips that last little bit to let her inner muscles grip him fully.

"Not too slow for you?" A fraction of an inch at a time, she did the same thing. Up, and then so satisfyingly down.

"Oh, no." She could see his fists grabbing great bunches of the velvet beneath him. Every muscle tensed, furrows in his forehead, beads of sweat on his upper lip.

"I thought you wanted me to hurry up so you could touch me." She took the next stroke a fraction of a second faster.

Jack bit his lip. "I was wrong." He gripped the curtain. She could see his knuckles were white. "God, that feels good."

Still at the top of her stroke, she leaned forward so her breasts were close to Jack's face. He lifted his head to her and suckled on one nipple, drawing its swollen peak into his mouth, making her gasp with pleasure.

Down, her breast still in Jack's mouth. His teeth closed gent-ly round her and she moaned and quickened her movements.

She'd never been totally in control like this. Jack's pupils were dilated, his mouth was wet and eager. She could feel every nuance of friction. It was building, faster now, into something huge and nearly unbearable between them. She shifted back so she was upright, let her hair tumble around her shoulders and watched him watching her move. Revelled in the admiration in his eyes.

"I dreamed about this," Jack said. She felt the vibration of his voice deep in his chest where her hands rested on him.

"Oh, me too," she gasped. She moved quickly now, all of her restraint gone. Every nerve in her body was driving her toward her climax in a dizzying rush.

"It was different. We were in a bed. And I was touching you." His words came in breathless bursts with their movements. Kitty only heard them distantly. Pleasure was curling its tendrils around her, growing, insisting.

"And you said different things. But it felt so good, like this, Kitty. And when you came, you yelled out—"

"Jack!" Kitty threw her head back and shuddered with the ecstasy that pulsed through her. She contracted around him and then felt Jack's final thrusts, the pleasure reaching an even higher peak. He lifted his hips up off the floor and her with him, and then he exploded inside her, crying her name upwards to the huge starry space above them.

Limp and overwhelmed, Kitty collapsed forward over his chest, and rose and fell with his ragged breathing. She twined her fingers in his damp hair and kissed him again. "Jack."

Right now, for this moment at least, hers at last.

"Kitty." His breath fluttered in her hair, his heart pounded against her breast. "That was the best I have ever felt."

She smiled.

"Now, please," she murmured, "I'd like you to hold me."

He lifted his hands from his sides and wrapped his arms around her, pressing her closely to him, brushing her hair back from her face.

Surrounded by Jack, enveloped in Jack, with the taste of Jack on her lips and her heart beating to the same time as his, Kitty closed her eyes and drifted toward the sleep that had eluded her last night.

Her dreams were going to be so good.

CHAPTER NINE

SOMEWHERE, a phone was ringing.

Jack opened his eyes. The first thing he saw was the glorious fire of Kitty's hair, spread out on his chest. Every curl a caress.

Her limbs were entangled with his, her pale skin a rich contrast with his tanned body. Her face rested on his shoulder. Her eyes were closed and her pink lips smiled slightly. He remembered their last kiss, drenched in satisfied passion, and he felt desire stir in him.

The phone rang again.

Gently, reverently, Jack cradled Kitty's head in his hand and placed it on the curtain. Then he extricated himself from her embrace and stood.

The phone rang again. It sounded muffled and far away. Kitty didn't wake, only breathed deeply once and then curled herself into a graceful S-shape on the velvet.

Without her skin near him, the air seemed colder. Jack listened for the direction of the phone. That way, in the lobby. He padded up the aisle and walked through the light trap.

The ringing stopped. He stood there, in the doorway, straining his ears to hear it again. Maybe it was from another building?

It rang again, nearly making him jump. It sounded closer now, and slightly below him. Jack crept forward.

Now, standing in the center of the lobby, he could tell it came from below him. He followed the sound until he was standing at the edge of the trapdoor. Gently, so as not to make any noise, Jack lifted the door.

It was definitely down there.

He gingerly lowered himself down into the hole, wincing as the splintery sides dug into his hands and scratched against his naked thighs. A step down from the velvet chair and he was there.

His cell phone lay next to a big box of letters for the marquee. Right where he must have put it, and forgotten it, two or three days ago when he was exploring around. He hit the answer button. "Hello?"

"Hi, Jack. How's the cycling trip going?" Gene Taylor's deep, cheerful voice filled his ear.

"Hi, Dad." Jack kept his voice low. "It's—incredible."

"Some weather, huh?"

Jack glanced around the dusty, airless hole. "Yeah."

"Your mother's out gardening already. It feels like July. Too hot for cycling?"

"Um, no. It's been fine."

And, Dad, do you think you could drive over to the Delphi and let me and Kitty out of here?

He didn't say it.

"Your mother is incredibly proud of you, you know. We had the bridge club over last night and she was showing everybody that article about you and the Delphi."

Speaking of the Delphi, I'm locked in it.

"I'm glad she's proud of me," Jack said.

"We both are. I always knew that you'd accomplish something extraordinary once you put your whole mind and heart into it."

"Thanks. Um, Dad?"

"Yes?"

"I need your help."

"Anything, Jack. What is it?"

The words that came out weren't the ones he was planning to say.

"Have you ever had a dream that came true? I mean an actual dream? That you had while you were sleeping?"

"You mean like your grandmother Taylor, the stage psychic? No, not me."

"Do you really think Grammy was psychic?" Jack asked.

Gene chuckled. "Well, she always knew when I was up to mischief, but, then again, so did your mother with you. Why do you ask?"

"Oh. No reason." Jack rubbed his forehead with his hand and tried to dispel the weird feeling that had settled over him. His parents were proud of him. He wasn't telling his father the truth. And his dreams were coming true.

"Well, I hope the rest of your trip is good. Come for dinner Monday night if you're back in time."

"Okay. Thanks. Um—hey, Dad?"

"Yes, Jack?"

"I'm stuck—" The words caught in his throat.

Kitty only wanted their relationship to last as long as they were locked in. If he told his father, he'd lose Kitty as soon as the Delphi door opened.

"Jack? What is it?"

He swallowed. "I'm glad you're proud of me."

"You deserve it, son." Gene hung up.

Jack stared at the phone in his hand. Even though it must have been lying here for days, it still had some charge in it. Enough to call anyone: police, locksmith. His father again, and tell him the truth.

He stepped on the velvet chair and pulled himself up to floor level. Then he went back into the cinema and down the aisle toward the stage. Kitty hadn't moved. Her shoulder and hip made gentle curves of white skin against the darkness of the wood-panelled wall behind her. Jack stood, the phone in one hand, and looked at her.

God, she was so beautiful. Her arm lay across her breasts, but he could see the swell of them moving with her breathing, and the top of one rosy nipple. He remembered the feeling of her smooth thighs gripping him, her body collapsed on top of his. How wonderful their lovemaking had been.

And he hadn't even touched her yet. Not really. Not as he wanted to.

He looked at the phone. There was a good, strong signal up here. He'd call someone and get them rescued. It was the decent thing to do, and no matter what Kitty seemed to think, Jack was a decent guy. He'd tell her about the phone and he'd call a locksmith and they could get out of here and he'd never make love with her again.

He'd call. As soon as he'd touched Kitty. Just once.

He put the phone down on one of the seats and knelt down, feeling the warmth from her body. Or maybe his own body was simply responding to the nearness of her. He was definitely responding in other ways just from looking at her—just as he had from the moment they'd first met again.

No, having an erection near Kitty was nothing new. But this warmth just from being close—where did that come from?

Jack reached out his hand and let it hover over the swell of her hip. A whisper away from touching. His palm skated upward over her side, his fingers just above her skin, following every dip and curve. Heat crept up his arm and flushed through his body.

Amazing. He'd never felt that before. It was him reacting to her.

Jack swept his hand over her shoulder, down her arm. It was almost touching, a tease. But he was also learning her now, while she was still asleep. Here on her arm his fingers brushed against the soft blond hairs. And then he travelled over the feminine bones of her wrist, up and down each hill of her knuckles, along the talented hand that could capture a vision on paper.

He lifted his hand to her face and nearly caressed her features, examining each part of her as he traced it. Her eyelids, so delicate and translucent they were almost blue over her eyes. The fine arch of eyebrow and the perfect line of her nose. A small scar at its bridge he'd never noticed before.

He knew how her cheeks would feel, and the moist silk of her lips, because he'd kissed them. But this almost-touch taught him more, let him understand better how her few freckles made the paleness of her skin even more exquisite. How her lips met each other in a soft kiss. How the little smile lines at their corners had been etched there by her happiness and her laugh.

And then there was her hair. Jack couldn't hold himself back any longer; he plunged his fingers into its depths and let it curl around him. It was warm, heavy, perfumed with vanilla and Kitty. He held it in handfuls and felt the fire in him growing even hotter. Kitty opened her eyes. "Hello," she whispered.

"Hello." He bent to brush a kiss over her lips. Just as sweet as he remembered.

"Have we been rescued yet?"

"Not yet. Thank God."

In a minute. He'd tell her in a minute. He hadn't touched her enough yet.

He slid one hand out of her hair to rest on the side of her neck. Her pulse thrummed against his fingers. "It's okay to touch you now?"

Kitty nodded. The movement shook a lock of hair loose and over her face, hiding her eyes.

"Kitty?" Jack pushed the lock aside. Her eyes were lowered, not meeting his. "You're not regretting this, are you?"

She bit her lip, and he saw she was thinking it over.

She had to think it over? Panic stabbed him in the gut.

"Don't regret it, Kitty. Please don't regret it. It was incredible. Wonderful. Amazing. The best—"

At that word, she suddenly raised her eyes to his. As always, they made him dizzy. "The best I have ever felt," he finished.

"I don't regret it," she said softly. "I wanted you. I've always wanted you. And—" a smile tilted her lips "—it was pretty darn good, wasn't it?"

Relief hit him as hard as the panic had. He wasn't sure if he'd ever grinned quite so widely. "I'm not sure if it can get any better. But we can try."

She raised a hand to his chest and raked her fingers lightly through the hair there. "I've never done anything like that. Given orders. Made rules. Stood back and looked." She traced the contours of his ribs. "You're beautiful, you know."

Jack was intrigued. He'd been so wrapped up in the way she made him feel, that he hadn't really thought about how he made her feel. "Why could you act differently?"

She narrowed her eyelids as she thought; it only made the green of her eyes more intense. "I'm not sure. This place, maybe. Dreams come true in this cinema. Like you said the first time you showed it to me."

"Oh, you were listening to me that day? I thought you thought I was insane."

"No. You were right. This is that sort of place. Because it was a dream of mine, Jack, making love to you. It has been, for as long as I can remember. Of course—" her eyes glinted with mischief "—when I was sixteen my fantasies weren't quite so...explicit."

Jack laughed. "Mine were."

"Somehow I'm not surprised."

He couldn't help touching her smile with his fingers. "But this is better than any fantasy. Better than a dream."

Even better than *that* dream.

"Why?" she asked.

He thought about it for a minute. "I don't know. It's different. It's more complicated, and that makes it better. Maybe because it's real."

She smiled. "I bet your dreams usually come true. You're that type of person."

"I never really thought about it. But I know one dream that I can make come true now. Can I touch you?"

Kitty stretched out luxuriantly on the velvet. "Oh, yes, please." Her movement left her body exposed to him, her breasts uncovered by her arm, her thighs slightly parted. His eyes travelled down her, and his mouth went dry.

"I don't know where to start," he whispered.

"Start wherever you like." Her smile was languorous, her eyes heavy-lidded. All of the doubts she'd had were banished, he could tell. She'd decided to give herself up to pleasure and to him. For now, at least.

"What if we were about to get rescued?" he asked.

She laughed. "Then you'd better hurry up." She caught his hand in hers and brought his fingers to her lips. In turn, she gave each of his fingers a butterfly kiss. Then a warm, moist kiss on his palm. She guided his hand down over her smooth cheek, the line of her jaw, down her neck to her collarbone. "Now, go wherever you want."

God, he wanted to go everywhere and do everything. To touch all of her at once, and to explore slowly inch by inch. To look and look and never stop looking, and to stop looking and let his fingers and his skin only feel. To crush her to him so they were as close as two people could be, and to stay apart from her like this, and only brush her with his fingertips.

To squeeze everything he'd dreamed of and everything he wanted into this one time, while it lasted.

Just this once. And then he'd get them rescued. And then it would never happen again, but he'd have the memories as well as his dreams.

"And here I thought you were impatient to touch me." Kitty's voice, laced with humor, brought him back to himself and made him realize that he was kneeling, hand on Kitty's collarbone, without having moved at all.

He frowned. "I was. I am. But I think this is the first time in a very long time that I haven't quite known what to do with a woman."

Kitty's expression was half-comical, half-wry. "I'm not sure if that's a compliment or what."

"Oh, it is." He leaned forward to kiss the swell of the top of her breast. "Believe me, it really is."

And then he couldn't stop his hands. He filled them with Kitty. He knelt beside her and stroked her skin and dipped his head to her and smelled her scent. He moulded his hands around her hips and felt how perfectly they fit. He tasted the velvet skin of her belly and heard her exhale shakily.

"I can't believe how gorgeous you are," he said against her ribs. He watched his hand skate upwards and curve itself around the sweet weight of her breast. His thumb brushed her nipple, and she gasped.

"I've been dying for you to touch me since I first saw you again," she breathed. "Every time you looked at me I could imagine your hands on me."

"I know exactly what you mean." He touched his tongue to the peak of her nipple and then blew on it softly, watching it harden further. Amazing. "You wouldn't believe the things I've imagined doing with you."

"I think I can."

"Can't have. You would have slapped me." He glanced up at her face, a grin on his lips.

She smiled back. "I nearly did, a couple of times."

"Oh, yes. I remember." Slowly, enjoying every flavor and texture, he licked around the soft rounded flesh of her breast, and sucked her nipple wholly into his mouth. She hissed and arched against him, tangling her fingers in his hair and pressing him closer. He let his teeth scrape against her and felt her shudder.

Jack silently thanked God for providing women, and especially Kitty, with two breasts—one for his mouth, and one for his hand. He explored both of them fully, hearing her breathing speed up and the little whimpering noises she made increase in volume. Her hips shifted restlessly; Jack, not breaking contact with her breasts, stretched out beside her and lay his leg over hers, feeling her smooth thigh pressing against him where he was, again, hard and throbbing with need. She moved her leg, caressing his erection, and the need became even more urgent.

But not so urgent that he couldn't wait until he had tasted all of her. He lifted his mouth from her nipple and kissed a hungry trail down her stomach. He stopped halfway and looked up at her face. Her cheeks were flushed, her eyes gleaming underneath heavy lids.

"Did you imagine me here?" He slipped his tongue into her navel, and her stomach quivered.

"Oh, yes."

The curls between her legs were silky and flaming red. He planted a kiss just above them, and spread his fingers out over them. "Did you imagine me here?" Her hair trembled with his breath.

"I especially imagined you there."

He raised an eyebrow at her. Saw her smile at him in return. "I'll show you what I imagined," he said, and dipped his head between her legs.

Her moan was low, guttural, saturated with desire. With his lips in slow kisses, with his tongue in languid licks, with his teeth in gentle nibbles, Jack devoured the essence of Kitty.

The most delicious taste he had ever tasted.

He'd done this with other women. Of course he had. But never like this. He felt as if he were giving Kitty a gift. As if every stroke were another little present of pleasure. Pleasure that built in him, too. Her movements, her taste, her moans, created a haze of delight that surrounded him. Bubbled up inside him. Made him want to smile.

He did smile, never stopping his caresses. He couldn't help it. He was happy.

"Jack." Kitty's groan was urgent; he could tell from the sound of her voice that she was close to her climax. He stilled his tongue on her and savored her. Kitty whimpered and moved her hips eagerly—he could feel her impatience, the driving force of her passion, in every inch of her he touched. In the air around them both. He placed his hands on her hips and held her still.

He needed to look in her eyes when she came. He needed to see that green become darker, promise everything to him. After a last long, leisurely lick, Jack kissed back up her body, lingering at tempting spots along the way. Her hip bone, a beautiful peak beneath her thin skin. The side of her breast. Her neck, bathed with her scent.

And then her mouth. Sweet, moist, like the most luscious honey. "Jack," she whispered, "please don't stop."

"I'll never stop, darling." The words fell from his lips without any thought. He felt her trembling, longing for release, and every fibre of his body wanted to give it to her.

He kissed her again and his hand went back between her legs. He slipped a finger inside her, oh, yes, so hot and wet, as close to heaven as you could get on earth. Kitty arched up against his hand and he found her clitoris and rubbed with his thumb, loving her gasps and the way her body undulated against him. She was nearly there.

Jack pulled his head back from hers and watched Kitty. Her eyes had fluttered shut and her brows were drawn down, as if she were concentrating all of her attention on the sensations he was giving to her. She bit her bottom lip and tensed, trembling, holding her breath. He stroked once again. And once more.

And then her eyes flew open and she grabbed him and her hips bucked against him. Her body convulsed, her breath came out in a long cry.

But it was her eyes that showed him her pleasure. He saw when they became unfocused. When their pupils expanded, and they stopped seeing anything but him and what he had made her feel. The moment when, briefly, Jack became her whole world.

The moment he'd been waiting for, for…how long?

He watched sense return to her eyes. They focused again and looked into his. Then Kitty smiled at Jack, pure joy beaming from her, and he'd been waiting for this moment, too.

"Do I deserve a slap for that?" he asked her.

"No, you deserve a medal." She pulled his head to hers with both hands and kissed him.

He was lost. He was crazy. This was something more than a year's abstinence catching up with him. There was no way that any other woman on the face of this earth could taste and feel and look as good as Kitty Giroux Clifford did, right now.

Then Kitty reached down and wrapped her fingers around the hard length of his erection and stroked him, every finger a separate exquisite friction, and he lost even the power of distracted thought.

His hands were shaking as he reached for a condom and got it out of the packet and onto him. And then he was there where he was meant to be, inside Kitty, her breath in his ear and her spring-green eyes looking into his, and all of his control was gone. He drove into her, fast and hard and wild and deep, feeling her legs wrap around his waist and her body meet his every thrust.

She was made for him. He was made for her. Both. Whatever. They fit, they belonged, they moved and breathed and thought to the same rhythm. He pushed one of her legs up onto his shoulder and saw her eyes widen as he plunged even deeper within her. As close as two human beings could be.

Until they both reached the edge together, clung desperately to each other, and tumbled over. At that moment the whole world disappeared, and there was only him and Kitty. Eyes burning. Bodies joined.

Complete.

It felt like forever before he was able to see straight again. The first thing he could focus on was Kitty's shoulder. He was leaning his chin against the hollow of it and his nose was nearly touching her. There were five freckles across the top of her shoulder, making a "W" shape on the creamy skin, like the constellation Cassiopeia.

He shifted his weight so he was lying next to her and curled his arms and legs around her. He felt the sweat cooling on his body and the heat of where he touched her. Jack cradled Kitty's face in his hand.

"You've got Cassiopeia on your shoulder."

"Really?" Her voice was husky, sated.

"Really."

"I think that's the strangest thing anyone has ever said to me after making love."

"I'm glad I'm memorable." He kissed her damp forehead.

"Oh, you are." Kitty laced her fingers with his.

Jack buried his face in her hair. Had he ever been so happy? He drifted on a cloud of bliss, vanilla-scented and the color of flame.

And then he remembered the phone. The phone that would rescue them from this heaven.

His eyes flew open.

Wait. Hold on. This couldn't end. Not when it was just starting. Not when he'd found out how happy she could make him.

Kitty's stomach growled, and it gave him an idea.

"Hungry?" He lifted his head and looked at her with what he hoped was nonchalance.

"Yeah. I could kill a box of Raisinets just now."

"You know what I could kill?" He spread his hand out on her stomach. "Two eggs, bacon and home fries."

She groaned. "And stacks and stacks of buttered toast. Don't talk about it."

His index finger made circles around her belly button. "Chico at Bob's Diner down the road makes the best breakfast in Portland. I'll treat you."

"Stop torturing me."

"No, I will. As soon as we get out of here. A huge plate, with everything you ever wanted for breakfast on it. And coffee. And juice. And all the buttered toast you can eat." He felt her stomach grumble again, under his hand. "And then we'll go back to my house. We can take a long, hot shower together. We can get into my bed. And I can show you everything else I want to do with you."

Kitty closed her eyes. She was going to say yes.

Jack wondered who he should call first—his dad, or a locksmith.

She opened her eyes, smiled, and shook her head. "You're very tempting. But sorry, no. I made some rules, remember? Once we get out of here, we work together, and that's it." She walked her fingers down his forehead, down his nose, over his lips and to his chin. "Let's just enjoy this while it lasts, okay?"

While it lasts. Which could be half an hour more, if he called. Or maybe about thirty-six hours, if he didn't tell Kitty about the phone and they waited until Oz got back from Canada, or their parents called the police.

"Are you sure?" he asked.

"Jack, it's not a question of being sure. It's what's going to happen."

A lot could happen in thirty-six hours. He could make love with Kitty some more. He could talk to her. He could learn more about her. He could show her how happy he could make her.

And, maybe, he could find the clue that would persuade her that this didn't have to end.

He kissed her cheek, hard. "I'll go get the Raisinets."

Jack picked up the phone, hiding it in his hand, and went up the aisle to the lobby. He was more careful going down through the trapdoor this time, and didn't graze his skin. He turned the phone off, put it next to the box again and covered it with some rags. Then he climbed back up and closed the door.

I guess this officially makes me a jerk after all, he thought, grabbing two boxes of chocolate-covered raisins from the concession stand.

The thing was, being a jerk was the better choice. Guilt, he could deal with. Losing Kitty, he couldn't. And once she learned that they were meant to be together, she'd thank him for not telling her about the phone.

Someday, they'd laugh about this. He was certain of it.

Almost.

CHAPTER TEN

"TELL me about yourself." Jack popped a chocolate-covered raisin into Kitty's mouth, and she took the opportunity to nip at his finger. "Tell me everything. Don't leave anything out."

Kitty reached for the candy box and looked at Jack doubtfully. "Everything? That would be pretty boring."

"You could never be boring. I bet you've had a fantastic life. Mixing with the rich and famous in Los Angeles, designing their houses. Wowing everyone with your talent. Men walking a thousand miles for a mere touch of your glorious film-star hair. I would."

"You'd have to walk around the Delphi a lot of times before you got to a thousand miles."

Kitty ate another raisin. Fantastic life among the rich and famous. People impressed by her talent. Yeah, right. That had been the way she'd imagined LA would be like, too, in her wildest dreams. The reality had been quite substantially different. A failed marriage, a job with a company she'd liked, but which had ultimately been a compromise. It had been a relief to escape back to Maine.

"Here, catch." She tossed a raisin toward Jack, and he caught it in his mouth. "If you want to know everything about me, you'll have to give me something in return."

"And what might that be?" He licked his lips suggestively.

Kitty giggled. "I sort of had the feeling that you'd be giving me that anyway, at the soonest possible opportunity. I meant something else."

Jack's grin was so gorgeous she wanted to laugh, or scream, or something. "You mean you want to know everything about me, too? I thought you knew everything about me already. I'm a feckless ne'er-do-well, a womanizing fool who doesn't know the meaning of the word 'commitment'. Right?"

Right. But she'd decided not to think about any of that right now. "I meant that I want to draw you."

His surprise was evident. "Draw me? Sure. Can I ask why?"

Good question. Her request had been an impulse, but, now that she thought about it, she knew why she had asked it. It was partly a way of learning him, seeing his body and his face and his personality in a different way. Maybe, by committing the lines of his body onto paper, she could capture him in a way she could study. Somehow, it might help her understand Jack better.

And of course, the drawing would be a reminder of their time here together. Something she could look at and think about after all of this was over. The only permanent thing to come out of this affair.

She didn't know whether she'd be able to look at it afterward, of course. Kitty suspected that after they left the Delphi any reminder of these precious limited hours was going to be far too painful to consider. But she wanted the drawing enough to take the risk of future pain.

She wasn't going to say any of those things, though. "Professional pride. I'm a much better artist now than I was in high school when I did my last drawing of you."

"Funny, I never thought of you as vain. I mean, don't get me wrong, you have reason to be, but I never dreamed that underneath that modest exterior there lurked a huge ego."

She swatted him with the box of Raisinets. "If I didn't know you were joking, you'd be wearing this box where the sun don't shine."

He raised one eyebrow. "Mmm, kinky."

Kitty laughed. "I'm not vain. I'd just like to do a better drawing, that's all."

"I understand. It's tough to be judged on what you were like in high school. I mean, people change a lot when they grow up."

Kitty stared.

"So where do you want me?"

Kitty was far too confused to appreciate the *double entendre.* "Wherever you feel comfortable. I'll go get some paper."

She picked up Jack's sweatshirt from where she'd discarded it and pulled it on, despite his little noise of disappointment. It was harder to think when she was naked. Leaving Jack still sprawled over the curtain, she went into the lobby to get her sketch pad and pencils.

Jack Taylor: dickhead or darling? High-school heartbreaker or grown-up heartthrob? He was the best lover she'd ever had—okay, that wasn't saying much, as she hadn't exactly had many—but was he capable of love? Did he even know what love was?

Did she?

She picked up her sketch pad, and took advantage of the fact that Jack couldn't see her to shake her head and give herself a good talking-to.

Stupid Kitty. Stupid, naïve, vulnerable, desperate Kitty. Why was she thinking about love? She'd decided to limit the time of their affair precisely so she wouldn't have to think about love, so she wouldn't have to risk her heart.

And she knew Jack Taylor as well as she needed to. She knew how wonderful his lovemaking was—no, not merely wonderful. Spectacular. Mind-blowing. All-encompassing.

She knew that he was passionate, and intense, and funny, and tender. Charming and generous. Confident and visionary.

But she also knew what Jack Taylor was like when it came to relationships. In fact, he'd said it himself. *A feckless ne'er-do-well who didn't know the meaning of the word "commitment".*

Whatever "feckless" meant.

Who was she kidding, thinking that drawing him was going to let her know him any better than she did already?

She wanted that drawing, though. Wanted to trace the contours of his body on paper. Wanted to capture the sparkle in his brown eyes, that sexy uplift of his smile.

In fact, she seemed to be nothing more than a big bundle of wants lately.

Paper and pencils in hand, and nothing settled in her head, she went back to Jack. He had sat up and was leaning against the wall, one leg stretched out in front of him and one leg bent at the knee. A position that afforded her a very good view of his sculpted chest and his crotch—not fully aroused now, but magnificent nevertheless. Suddenly, she wanted to trace his body with a lot more than her pencil.

But the pencil could come first. Then…all the other things could come afterward.

She chose a seat in the front row and put the paper and pencils down in front of it. Then she picked up her jeans from the floor.

"Hold on," said Jack. "I never would have agreed to this if I'd known you'd have to put your clothes back on to do it. What on earth are you getting dressed for?"

"The dust sheet is dirty," she pointed out. "The idea of getting my bare butt covered in dust is less than appealing."

"I'd clean the dust off your butt. That's pretty appealing."

It was, but now that she had her jeans on again she felt a little bit more in control of her thoughts. "What if somebody comes in? I'd rather have my clothes on if that happened."

Jack laughed. "But it's okay for me to be stark naked? Thanks."

"Well, half the female population of Portland has probably seen you naked anyway, so what have you got to lose?"

He shook his head. "I'm glad you think I'm such a stud, but I think you're overestimating numbers. I'm not that feckless. What do you want me to do while you draw me?"

She settled herself on the chair and opened her sketchbook. "Nothing special. Just talk." Kitty began to sketch.

"Can you talk and draw at the same time?"

"Yeah."

"Good. I can start to learn everything about you. Tell me about yourself."

"What's to tell? I'm twenty-seven. I was born in Portland, and I moved to LA to go to college, and I moved back here eight months ago. I've got a brother and a mother, and a father I haven't seen for fifteen years. I'm an interior designer. My favourite color is bright pink, and I can't wear it because I've got red hair. There isn't much to learn about me, really."

"I think there is. I'm intensely curious about you, Katherine Giroux Clifford."

The contours of his shoulder and his neck had taken shape underneath her pencil. She looked up at him and examined the hollow of his collarbone, how dark hair began at the base of his neck. "What are you curious about?"

"Lots of things. For example, ever since we talked about high school I've been wondering why, if you had a crush on me for three years, you never once talked to me. Why didn't you even say hi until I crept up behind you in art class?"

Kitty knew the answer to that question; she'd thought about it nearly every day of her high-school existence. "I was a skinny kid with frizzy red hair and braces who wore geeky second-hand clothes."

"You weren't geeky. You were pretty. I like red hair."

"You were the most popular boy in your class and you hung out with Oscar Strummer, the smartest person in the whole school. There was no way you were going to notice me."

"But you sat in the same art room with me for six months and drew me and never said hi. You can't have been that shy."

"It wasn't just shyness. You were out of my league, Jack. Let's put it this way: where did you come from?"

"California. Why?"

"I never even left Maine until I was seventeen and I borrowed my mother's car to drive across the bridge into New Hampshire to see if it was any different. Where did you live when you came to Portland? What was your house like?"

"We lived on Peak's Island. My dad designed the house. It was always Dad's dream to build his own house out of local materials, near the ocean."

"Me and Marie went to the island and walked past your family's house once. It's gorgeous, Jack. Huge. All that glass and granite and warm pine."

She traced the line of his jaw, making it more solid.

"You've been to the house I grew up in," she said. "For as long as I can remember it's been falling down. We never had any money to replace anything, so we repaired it as best we could. When I was a kid, every month we'd get the duct tape out and tape everything back together: the couch, the linoleum in the kitchen, the broken window in my brother's bedroom. Mom used to call it 'Duct Tape Day' and pretend it was a special occasion."

"Your mother's house looked fine when I visited," Jack said.

"That's because you only saw the kitchen, and I redid that for Mom's birthday. With both of us kids grown up she could finally spend some money getting stuff fixed, but she doesn't. All the plumbing is still held together with duct tape. My mother is a receptionist in a vet's office. After my dad skipped town for good, she had to support both of us kids on her salary alone. What does your mother do?"

"She hasn't got a job, but she does a lot of charity work."

"She picked you up from school one time and I saw her while I was waiting for the bus. She was beautiful. Her clothes were the most elegant things I'd ever seen. My mom thinks spending more than twenty dollars on an item of clothing is a total waste of money."

Jack ran his hand through his hair, and Kitty erased a bit of what she'd drawn so she could capture the way a black lock now fell over his forehead. "You can't mean that you were intimidated by my family's house and my mother's clothes," he said. "If you were as in love as you said you were, surely that stuff wouldn't matter."

"Jack, you can say that because you had the beautiful house and the beautiful family and the perfect life. All that stuff matters if you don't have it. Believe me."

She hadn't stopped drawing the whole time she'd been talking, but with Jack's silence she stopped and looked up at his face. He was watching her intently.

"Does it still matter?" he asked.

She remembered her revelation at the barbecue: that her mother's house was much, much more precious than her perfect house had been. "Not so much. I've grown up, and I'm proud of what my mother achieved on her own. But you seem to take money for granted, and that can be pretty intimidating to someone who doesn't. How did you get the money to invest in the Delphi, if you don't mind me asking?"

Jack shifted position, but she'd already drawn his pose. She concentrated on his eyes and mouth as he spoke. "After I finished college I got in on an Internet company with a friend of mine," Jack said. "It was the right time, the right place, we made a killing. I got sick of it after a few years and sold out my share. Again, right time and place. I made enough so I didn't have to work again if I didn't want to. But I decided to buy the Delphi instead."

Kitty shook her head resignedly. "See? You've been so successful that you can afford to throw a career away and risk everything. Success is second nature to you."

"What about you, Kitty? You look like you're doing pretty well yourself, now. You've got a brand-new Mercedes and a top-of-the-range camera. I bet your clothes cost a lot more than twenty dollars an item. You've got a good career. Money and success can't matter between us anymore."

Between us? Jack Taylor, the Playboy of Portland, was talking about an "us"? The implausibility of it all made her laugh aloud.

"Jack, I haven't got any career. The Delphi is the only substantial work I've been offered since I came to Maine. I bought my car and my camera and my clothes and my phone and laptop and everything else while I was in California and I was getting paid a good salary with a design firm. I was living with Sam, and he insisted my salary was for my own use. When we split, I wanted him to keep what had been his already, which was the house and pretty much everything in it. As soon as the divorce was final I quit my job and moved out here to start my own business.

"I had an office and my own apartment at first, and I spent a lot of money on advertising. When I wasn't getting any business and I realized my savings were running out, I moved in with my mother. Right now I'm running the whole business—what there is of it—out of my mother's sewing room."

Keeping her eyes on her drawing made all of this easier to say to him. She filled in the dark of his eyes and his hair with vehement strokes. "If the Delphi hadn't come along, I was going to have to sell the car. And the next step was to work for someone else, and give up my dream of running my own design firm. So it does matter, Jack." She raised her eyes and met his, feeling, somehow, both utterly vulnerable and utterly strong.

"That's one reason why we can't let this affair go beyond this weekend," she said. "Restoring the Delphi means too much to my career for me to risk it by fooling around with its owner. Do you understand?"

In an instant Jack was off the curtain and was kneeling in front of her. God, when he was a few feet away and she was looking at him in pieces, to draw him, he was manageable. But here, close, naked, the heat and scent of his body reminding her of the pleasure they had shared—that was something else.

"Kitty." He took her hand, removed the pencil from it and held it in both of his. "No amount of fooling around that we can do will jeopardize your job restoring the Delphi. That is completely secure, no matter what happens between us. You're the one that I want for the Delphi. I knew that the minute I saw your designs. And the fact that the minute that I saw you, I wanted you, too..."

He trailed off, creased his forehead. "I can't say it's separate, because it isn't. But I can promise you that you'll be the only designer working on the Delphi. Nobody else could do it."

His brown eyes were so sincere. His face was so expressive. She had learned that Jack Taylor could keep his promises. For whatever reason he gave them. She nodded.

"And your success, or your lack of it up till now, doesn't mean anything to me," he continued. "I've got total belief in your abilities. You've captured my vision for the Delphi with a few lines of your pencil. Hell—" he looked down at her drawing that lay beside him on the floor "—you've captured *me* with a few lines of your pencil. I'm beginning to think that in some ways you know me a lot better than I know myself."

She nearly burst out laughing. "How can I know you better than you do yourself?"

He wound his fingers around hers and stroked the back of her hand with his thumb. Even that simple touch sent shivers of desire through her.

"What you said just now about my life. It *has* been easy. I've been successful at a lot of things without trying very hard at them. Oz always says that I skate through life, and you've made me see he's right. I never realized that from the outside my life probably does look perfect. So perfect that someone who really liked me never felt that she could get close. I'd never thought of that before."

Now this was a new concept for Kitty.

"You mean it's possible that you can be so lucky that you don't even realize that you're lucky? Boy, I wish I had a problem like that. Bad luck follows me around like a cloud."

Jack sat down in the seat beside her, still holding her hand. He didn't mind getting a dusty butt, she noticed. "What do you mean?"

"If something can go wrong for me, it will. It's been happening for years."

"Surely not everything has gone wrong for you."

"Pretty much everything. My dad left us when I was thirteen and it tore my world apart. So the first thing I did to fill that emotional void was to fall in love with the most unobtainable boy in the whole school, who dumped me on prom night. Much to the amusement of the rest of the school. I worked my butt off all through high school and missed out on being valedictorian by two points. I didn't get into my first choice of university because my application got lost in the mail, and I couldn't go to my second choice either because the financial-aid package wasn't good enough. I got offered a job at the second most prestigious design firm in LA after missing my interview at the first most prestigious firm because my condo caught on fire that day. I got married to a man who swore he'd love me forever and then after a year he left me for his first wife. Do you see any pattern here?"

"But those are all separate incidents. They can't possibly be connected."

Kitty shook her head. "Oh, yes, they are. By bad luck. I blamed you, you know. From the moment I saw you kissing Melissa Beauchamp, I've been doomed never to get what I want. I've tried. But it hasn't happened."

Kitty felt tears starting in her eyes. She bowed her head so that her hair would hide them.

It wasn't the past incidents of bad luck that she was crying about. Because she'd overcome them, she'd worked hard and she'd been strong.

It was this. Finally she could feel safe enough to tell somebody about all the failures of her life and how she felt about them—and that safety was only going to last for another day, at most.

Jack didn't say anything. He reached over to Kitty and pulled her over the armrest into his lap and wrapped his arms around her and hugged her, hard. Her cheek rested against his bare chest and she heard his heartbeat, steady and calming.

It was exactly what Kitty wanted.

A fat tear rolled down her face and dropped onto Jack's chest. She heard his breath catch and then her head was in both of his hands and she was looking him in the face.

He caught the second tear on her cheek with his lips, and the gentle kiss he pressed to her mouth was wet and salty. "I'm sorry," he said, and she felt the timbre of his voice vibrating through his body into hers and travelling all the way to the ends of her fingers and toes.

She sighed. "Don't say that, Jack. You were right yesterday; it's not your fault. I just wanted someone to blame, and you hurt me. And it was easier to blame you than my father. Or myself."

She wiped the last tears from her eyes and gave Jack a watery smile. "I've just got blind rotten luck sometimes. Like breaking off a stupid door handle and locking us in this cinema all weekend."

He smiled back. He was the most damn gorgeous man ever,

in the world. "That was the luckiest thing that has ever happened to me."

And then his kiss again, breathtaking and passionate and tender. Kitty held onto him tight. *Lucky,* she thought.

Or she tried to think it. But some doubt, some voice in the back of her mind was whispering, *Unlucky. Very, very unlucky.*

Jack's hands crept underneath the sweatshirt she was wearing and cradled her waist. His touch on her bare skin made her gasp. She shushed all the silly thoughts in her head and let herself enjoy the feeling of being fully clothed, in the embrace of a magnificent, gentle, caring naked man who happened to be the man she'd wanted more than anything for the past thirteen years.

Not fully clothed for long. Jack pulled the shirt up over her head and she wrapped her arms around his neck, and the feeling of her bare chest against his was so glorious.

"Stay with me," he murmured. "Don't let it end here. I feel so good whenever I touch you. Let's see where this leads us. Outside the Delphi."

Oh.

Her heart thumped a huge, painful thump. And she knew all at once where that voice whispering *unlucky* was coming from.

She loved him. She loved Jack. She'd never stopped loving him.

No. That wasn't right. She'd never stopped *wanting* him. The wanting had started the minute she'd seen him in that lunch line at high school. But that had been a crush on someone she didn't know. An airy nothing, a wish.

But this—what she felt right now—this was real, so big and so true that it caught in her throat and made her head feel like exploding. It had grown out of being with him. Out of touching him, out of talking with him, out of laughing with him. Out of sharing the same goals and the same pleasures. Out of the way she felt whenever he looked at her.

This feeling was something that made her teenage crush seem about as substantial as the dust bunnies in the corner of the theater.

And Jack, who was asking her to carry on this affair outside the safe realms of the Delphi? What did he feel? What on earth did he have to lose? Compared with her?

She wouldn't lose her job; he wouldn't let it happen. She believed that. But she could lose her heart. Forever. And Jack Taylor was not a man who treated hearts with careful hands. He didn't know how. He'd had an easy life. He hadn't fought the battles, or felt the pain, or been at the mercy of feelings that wouldn't go away no matter what you did.

He'd have a good time and then forget about her again. And she couldn't bear that. Not this time, when she had so much more reason to love him.

So she clung to him as tightly as she could. She kissed him and poured her soul into the kiss. She let her hands wander down his chest to where he was hard with desire for her again. She lifted her own hips and let him strip the jeans from her.

"Jack," she gasped as he encircled her waist and pulled her with him down onto the velvet curtain. "Let's enjoy this now. Don't spoil it by talking about what can never happen." She clung to him, pressed close. "Now, in this moment, while it's perfect. It might never happen again. Make love to me."

Jack groaned. And did as she asked.

CHAPTER ELEVEN

"AND then they walk off down the runway, into the rain, toward their new life." Jack pretended to turn up his collar, pull down his hat, and walked, smoking an imaginary cigarette, toward the end of the stage. "And the camera lifts and they get smaller and smaller as the French national anthem swells over a map of Africa and the words 'The End.'"

Kitty wiped her eyes. "Oh Jack," she sniffed.

Jack launched himself off the stage and landed in front of Kitty. "So, do you like it?"

"I didn't think it would be so sad. I thought movies always had to have happy endings. But when he sends her off to America, with her husband, even though he loves her and she loves him—"

Jack sat in the seat next to hers. "He has to. It's part of his moral redemption."

"I suppose. But..." She sighed. "Why don't you show me one with a happy ending, next?"

Jack shook his head and laughed, slumping back in his seat. "For God's sake woman, I just acted out all of *Casablanca* for you, including the German army occupying Paris and a full chorus of 'As Time Goes By.' Give me a rest."

She settled back, smiling. "Maybe you could show me another one tomorrow, if we don't get rescued first."

"Maybe." Jack's eyes shifted, and his expression changed.

Almost before she could notice it, and certainly before she could figure out what it meant, it had changed back. He grinned at her, his eyes sparkling.

"Maybe we could act out a few films ourselves. We could use that digital camera of yours to make our own blue movie."

"Ideas like that will get you slapped, after all."

Jack held his hands up in mock alarm. "Joking. I was joking. I'm not really a pig."

She could have sworn his eyes shifted a little bit when he said that, too, but again it was gone before she could fully register it. He curled a strand of her hair around one of his fingers and stroked to the end of it. She watched him watching it slip through his fingers. Then he lifted his eyes to hers.

"I don't want to get rescued," he said. "Do you?"

Surely he couldn't know the bolt of pure love and pure misery that shot through her when he said that. Surely he was joking again, talking about an affair that he thought they could enter into lightly. Another thing he could take up and play with and toss away easily when something better came along. As he had with his career, and all of his women.

He didn't look as if he was joking, though. He looked completely serious.

But there was no way that he could be.

Right?

Kitty swallowed and made herself smile. "Since it's completely out of our control, that's sort of a pointless question, isn't it?"

Jack opened his mouth as if to reply. Then he shut it. He dropped his hand from her hair and leaned away from her. "Yeah. You're right. It is pointless."

Kitty felt bereft. The easy, companionable mood that they'd shared was suddenly strained. She reached over and twined her fingers with his. "So," she said, in what she hoped was a light, cheerful voice, "I've told you a lot about myself, but there are still some things I don't know about you."

He smiled at her and she nearly sighed with relief.

"I doubt that. You seem to know everything about me. What do you want to know?"

"When did you know you loved the movies?"

In an instant, anything that had been distant or strange about him dropped away. A light came into his eyes; he seemed to be overflowing with energy again.

"It's not just the movies themselves. It's all this." He gestured to the building around them. For the hundredth time Kitty marvelled at the cinema: the intricacy of the gilded decoration, the richness of the velvet fabric, the intensity of every single silver star on the ceiling.

"My father's an architect and he took me and my mom to loads of great buildings when I was a kid. I guess I was about seven when we first went to the Bruin Theater in LA. Designed by S. Charles Lee, the master of cinema design. We saw a cartoon, I don't remember what it was about now. I didn't care what it was about. It was the place, the experience that hooked me."

"I'm surprised you didn't try to be an actor yourself," Kitty said.

Jack snorted. "Come on, you've seen me try to play Humphrey Bogart. I'm no actor."

"You were a wonderful Humphrey Bogart. You were a great Ingrid Bergman, too. You could have been an actor if you wanted to."

"No way," he said. "It would have been too much hard work. And I would have had to face a lot of failures."

The minute he said it, Jack's eyebrows shot up. "My God. That was it. I never thought about it before. I didn't want to work hard at it, and maybe fail. So I never tried."

It was sort of comical, this sudden self-discovery of Jack's.

But it was touching, too. With his enthusiasm about the movies and his surprise at his own words, he seemed almost like a kid again. Except there was something deeper in there, as well.

"You're certainly taking on a lot of hard work and risk of failure with the Delphi," she observed. "So you can't be too reluctant to try for something you really want."

"Oz said something a while back—the day I was down that hole, just before you came in. He said that I loved movies because my attention span only lasted about two hours and then I was ready for something new."

"Was he right?" she asked.

"I think he used to be. But things are changing. My parents said they were proud of me, this mor— The other day." His mobile face clouded for a moment, and then it cleared and he looked at her. "I've had a lot of success, but they've never called me up just to say they were proud of me before."

"It must have felt good."

"It did. It does," he said. Kitty watched him thinking.

"I'm changing how I'm feeling about things," he said. "The Delphi. And you." Jack cupped her face in his hands and caressed her lips with his thumbs. "I'm beginning to see how I could have an attention span that lasts a very long time."

His kiss was thrilling and close. Then he pulled back to look in her eyes again, and said, "Maybe even that lasts forever."

What was this feeling? Cold, hot, ecstasy, pain? She stopped breathing and her heart skittered.

Forever?

With Jack?

"Do you think it's possible?" he whispered. "Do things like that happen?"

"I don't know." It was just barely audible, squeezed out on the little bit of breath she had in her lungs. She wasn't sure what she was saying, her thoughts were still stalled in her head. Did he mean it? Had he changed that much? Could she even dare to hope?

"It—it happens in the movies," she said.

Jack kissed her again, gently. Then he stood and held out his hand to her.

"Come on," he said. "Let's feel what it's like to be in the movies."

She took his hand and he led her up the steps onto the stage in front of the movie screen. She made the mistake of looking toward the back of the cinema, straight at the projector, and the light dazzled her.

"Don't look up there," he said. "Look here. Look at me."

Jack, one side of his face cast into shadow, smiled slightly, watching her. "I always thought that film stars were beautiful. But you're the most beautiful woman I've ever seen, in real life or on the screen. Every time you smile at me it's like magic."

And every time he looked at her she *felt* like the most beautiful woman in the world. His eyes had a way of doing that to her.

"Do you remember the last really good film you saw?" he asked. "Do you remember what it felt like when the hero and the heroine finally kissed, on screen, the whole shot taken up by their faces?"

"I haven't seen that many movies," she said.

"Then I'll show you. Watch the screen." He took her in his arms and kissed her. And Kitty, her eyes on the screen beside them, saw their shadows made huge by the projector. The curls on her head, Jack tall above her, his shoulders making a protective curve toward her.

It was as if they were in the movies.

She helped Jack remove her shirt and she pulled off his, both of them watching themselves on the silver screen. She saw him bend and take her breast in his hand and his mouth. She saw her own throat silhouetted as she threw back her head in ecstasy. She tangled her hands in his hair and lifted his head to hers.

"That's incredible," she gasped.

He kissed her again, and then said, "Keep watching."

Jack's shadow bent down and kneeled before her. She saw the shadow of each of his fingers as he unfastened her jeans and slowly guided them down her legs. She watched him stand, and she watched herself remove his jeans and toss them aside. Then they both stood and looked at themselves projected onto the screen beside them. Naked and exposed for everything they were. But somehow, Kitty thought, more than what they were by themselves.

They both looked away from the screen and at each other at the same moment. She touched him and he touched her. Jack ran his hands down her sides, a slow, careful caress that made her tremble.

"I don't know what it feels like to be in love," he said to her. "I've only ever seen it in films. I've never tried it." His lips tilted up ruefully. "I probably wouldn't know love if it came up and bit me on the backside. How do you know? What's it like in real life?"

It's like this, Kitty thought. *It's like what's really happening right now.*

She couldn't say it, so she kissed his collarbone instead.

He captured her chin in his hand and made her look up into his eyes. "Were you in love with your husband?"

That was a safer question. She clasped her hands behind Jack's neck. "I liked him. We were close, we were good friends. We really cared about each other. I thought being married to him would make me happy."

"But were you in love with him?"

"I don't know," she said, and then realized that wasn't true. Jack's brown eyes searching hers made her tell the truth, or at least part of the truth. As risky as it was.

"No. I wasn't in love with him. It wasn't like how I'd felt about you. It wasn't everything wrapped up in one person. But I thought that that probably wouldn't happen again. I wasn't really sure I wanted that to happen again; it was too scary. I figured that Sam was good enough."

"But he wasn't."

"He wasn't." *He wasn't you.* "And I wasn't good enough for him. He never felt passionately about me, like the way he felt about his first wife. Which is why he went back to her."

"He was an idiot for letting you go." Jack's eyes dropped from her face and followed his hands as they travelled upward from her waist. They skimmed her breasts, sending shock waves through her body, and then rested on her shoulders. She felt his finger touch her lightly five times on her left shoulder.

"Cassiopeia. Look." He pointed to the ceiling of the cinema, and she saw the constellation glowing on the dark blue sky. "You're like the Delphi. You're a dream come true. You feel like the most amazing thing that's ever happened to me."

"Jack," she sighed. The words he was saying were so wonderful, and she wanted them so badly to be true, that she stepped forward and pressed herself against his body. His erection branded heat against her stomach. His arms went round her and held her tight.

She didn't want him to stop talking to her. She wanted to hear more, and she wanted to believe everything he said. But the only place she felt completely safe, completely secure, completely confident and able to believe that anything in the world that she wanted was hers—the only place she felt all that was in Jack's arms and lost in his kiss.

So she sought out his lips and kissed him and stopped him from talking. She thrust her tongue into his mouth and swore she could taste the sweetness of the words he'd just said.

She kissed him again and again, feeling a hunger that was something like desperation rising in her. Kitty bit Jack's lower lip and he groaned into her mouth and cupped her buttocks in his hands, lifting her against him. Needing to get even closer, Kitty twined her legs around his thighs and gasped when she felt the base of his erection parting her, rubbing against her sensitized flesh. So hard and hot on her where she was molten with wanting him again.

Jack moaned again and ground himself against her and Kitty cried out with the pleasure of it. She looked down and saw the dark swollen head of his penis on the white skin of her belly and how their bodies fit together below. The sight of it sent another dizzying wave of ecstasy through her. Her muscles tensed, focusing all of her energy and all of her thoughts toward the climax that was rapidly building in her. She let her panting mouth fall away from Jack's and felt her eyes flutter closed, shutting out everything but her and Jack.

"Don't close your eyes. Look. At the screen."

Jack's whisper made her open her eyes and watch. Their shadows writhed on the screen. She could see the outline of his beautiful body and how her own hair tumbled back from her head. And then she watched herself buck against him as her orgasm grabbed hold of her and shook her.

She collapsed against Jack, boneless, and he slowly let her down to rest on her feet. She kissed him again, but the desperation had disappeared with her climax. Instead, she felt confident. Safe. As if she had everything she wanted.

"What would you like to see?" she asked him.

His erection was still iron-hard against her stomach, and she felt it jump at her words.

"Kitty," he said, breathless, "whenever I'm looking at you I'm seeing exactly what I want to see."

It had worked. She believed him.

Kitty smiled, and from the way Jack's pupils dilated she knew it was a sexy smile. "I think I can do better, though," she murmured. "Watch."

She kissed a trail down his chest and stomach and knelt in front of him. His penis stood stiff, pointing upwards, moving slightly with his laboured breathing. She curled her fingers around its shaft and touched its head with her tongue.

Velvet skin, and so hot. Jack's groan was deep and guttural. She explored his contours with her tongue and lips and heard his inarticulate sounds of desire. She loved this. He had given her so much pleasure and now here he was in her hands and in her mouth, and she could give to him in return.

Kitty slid her lips down him slowly until she had taken as much as she could, and then she looked up at Jack's face. His eyes were wide, his mouth open and slack. "Kitty," he breathed, and she saw his gaze move to the screen beside them. Watching his face the entire time, she pulled back until only the tip of him was in her mouth. She imagined what he was seeing, what they looked like larger-than-life, in silhouette. She swirled her tongue around him and then took his length in her mouth again. And sucked.

Jack groaned even louder and plunged his fingers in her hair. He guided her, showing her how to move. And all the time they were huge on the screen, a show for just the two of them. She felt powerful, and at the same time as if she were offering herself to him.

"Come with me," he gasped, and drew her head away from him. He sank to the floor and sat with his legs straight in front of him, pulling her to him so that her legs were around his waist. He reached back and found a condom in the pocket of his discarded jeans, sheathed himself, and lifted her up and onto him, surging inside her.

She yelled out his name, grabbing hold of his shoulders and digging her fingernails into his flesh. He felt so right; he filled her as no one else had filled her before and made her feel better than anything else had ever done.

Kitty met his open mouth and kissed him. She wanted him to drive into her. To force all the doubts away and push her relentlessly to a mind-shattering orgasm, again and again and again.

But he didn't. He stayed still within her. His tongue played with hers, withdrawing and circling. Kitty writhed against him. "Jack," she entreated, but his strong hands held her hips and stopped her moving. And then he took his mouth away from hers.

"Look at us, Kitty. That's you and me up there. I'm never going to look at that screen again without seeing the two of us together."

She was never going to look at *any* movie screen without seeing them together. This one showed Jack lifting her so he slid out of her, then thrust back in, so slowly, and so big up there in shadow and light. She moaned.

"Look." His words, hot in her ear. "There we are. Anything is possible. Isn't it?" He lifted her again. She tensed her legs and pulled him into her harder, deeper. She was going to climax again, any moment now.

"Anything," she breathed. She would give him anything. He was everything.

Jack moved her slowly, despite her efforts. The orgasm that was so maddeningly close was spun out, became a thread of pleasure exquisitely thin and sharp.

"Anything," he repeated. "Even that someone like me can fall in love. Do you believe me?"

"Yes." And then the ecstasy overwhelmed her and she felt as if she were part of that image on the screen that rocked back and forth and tossed her head back and shuddered down to her toes.

Jack followed her. She watched him through the haze of her own bliss, the big movie-Jack and the real, hot, precious Jack who trembled against her and surrendered to his own climax with an outrush of breath and a final clenching of her close to him.

And she was there, cradled to him, feeling open and overwhelmed and totally happy. He held her head in his hands and made her look in his passion-sated eyes. "Let it happen. Please, Kitty. Let's explore this feeling. I've never felt anything like it before."

I have. I've felt it as long as I've known you. And the feeling had changed and grown, until it permeated every fibre of her body and every part of her soul.

And Jack had changed, too. He wasn't merely charming. He wasn't heartless. He was…he was Jack, the man she'd waited her life for. The man she'd always wished he would be.

He kissed her forehead and smoothed away her hair. "Please tell me you'll give us a chance. After we're rescued. Trust me."

Oh, yes. Please, please, please, yes. The wave of yearning that swept through her was even stronger than the climax she'd just had.

She couldn't think so close to him. Kitty lifted herself off Jack and stood.

"Kitty?" Jack's face was bewildered and hurt.

"It's okay. I'm—I'm going to get us some popcorn. I'm hungry. It's got to be like, what, midnight?" She pulled on her panties and her T-shirt.

He jumped to his feet and grabbed her hand. "But what about my question? I'm serious about this, Kitty."

"I know you are." She traced the furrows in his forehead with her free hand. "I need space for a couple of minutes. Let me think this through a little bit. When I get back with the popcorn I'll tell you my decision."

Jack scanned her face for a moment, not letting go of her hand. He looked vulnerable and worried. With a deep breath, he released her fingers.

"Okay. Just don't be long."

"I won't." She made her way down the steps and up the aisle, past all the empty seats that had been watching them.

"Extra butter on mine!" he called after her.

"I know."

She shut the door to the light trap behind her and leaned against it.

Jack really wanted her. Not just her body, but her. He thought he was falling in love with her. He wanted a *relationship* with her. The first relationship he'd ever wanted to have.

A little yelp of joy escaped her lips. Why was she *thinking?* She should be happy-dancing all over this damn building, whooping and singing "Hallelujah."

Kitty skipped over the parquet floor toward the concession stand. She gave the elegant lines of the tiled wall an impulsive caress. "Thank you, Delphi," she whispered.

Her brain snapped back into gear. What would happen once they got outside the Delphi? Sure, at this moment she was everything to Jack. Because there were only the two of them. What about when they were out, and Jack could have any woman he wanted again?

This place, their affair, was an extraordinary dream. Reality could never live up to it. Kitty could never compete with all of the other women in Jack's life.

But I love him.

And with that she realized that she didn't have a choice. She had to put her heart into Jack's hands because she couldn't do anything else. It was why the alarm bells had rung the first moment she'd seen him again—because Kitty had known that if he weakened her, if he showed her even the teensiest bit of his heart, she would lose all control. She would be his.

He had shown her his heart, here in this dusty building, lit up by the projector and the silver screen. He might have shown her the whole thing, or it might have been the teensiest bit. It didn't matter.

She was his.

Kitty looked at herself in the shiny chrome of the popcorn dispenser. Her eyes were wide. She looked scared.

Get a grip, Kitty, she thought. *It doesn't make a blind bit of difference whether you're scared. Chickening out isn't an option. This has gone way too far for that.*

Decisively, she grabbed a cardboard bucket and shoved it

into the machine, scooping up an enormous cloud of popcorn. She pumped butter over the top of it.

She was going to go back into that beautiful room and tell Jack Taylor that yes, she wanted to have a relationship with him. No matter how long it lasted. Or what the consequences were.

She squared her shoulders and walked back toward the door to the theater. Every step one step closer to her destiny, whatever that would be.

Maybe, she thought, *it'll even have a happy ending.*

Then the floor slid beneath her bare feet. She heard an explosive crack, a shrieking, splintering sound that echoed in the vast space. And then the Delphi let out a roar and there was nothing holding her up and she fell in a shower of popcorn through the dusty air.

CHAPTER TWELVE

JACK sat swinging his feet from the stage. His heels made a hollow "thunk" every time they hit the wooden panelling.

Why did she have to think it through? If she felt anything like how he felt, she wouldn't have to think. The idea of being without Kitty was like the idea of being without oxygen. What thinking was needed?

But maybe she didn't feel anything like how he felt?

Jack realized that he was chewing on his thumbnail. He pulled his thumb out of his mouth and wiped it on his bare leg.

He wished he'd had more experience with stuff like this. How was he supposed to know how she felt? She hadn't told him. He knew she'd had a crush on him in high school. But high school had been a long time ago. He'd been a whole different person back then.

And he knew, now, that a crush was something very different from what he felt. He was totally crazy about Kitty. Addicted to everything she said and did. Fascinated by her talents, blown away by her personality, desperate to soothe every hurt she had ever felt.

If that wasn't falling in love, then every movie he had ever seen, every song he had ever heard, and every book he had ever read had been lying.

He was chewing on his thumbnail again. Jack shoved his hands underneath his thighs and worried.

How were you supposed to make a woman fall in love with you? Had he been doing it right? Considering that he'd spent most of his life trying to make sure that women *didn't* fall in love with him, he probably wasn't very good at it. Maybe he'd made some mistakes. Hell, he must have made some mistakes, because if Kitty loved him she wouldn't be spending so long getting popcorn.

He thought back over the past few hours. Exactly where had he gone wrong?

Aside from not telling her about the phone. But that had bought them some time. And she couldn't know about that, anyway.

A splintering crash assaulted his ears. A scream, suddenly cut short. From the lobby. Where Kitty was.

Jack leapt from the stage, sprinted up the aisle, and burst through the door. Through the cloud of dust, he saw what had happened. A hole gaped in the floor. Only one jagged half of the trapdoor remained.

"Kitty!"

He ran to the side of the hole and dropped to his knees. "Kitty?"

Oh, please don't let her be hurt. His entire body and mind screamed it. He couldn't see through the dust for a moment, and panic froze him.

Then he heard her moan and he jumped into action. A step down onto the chair and he could see her in the shadows, lying on her side on the ground. Her bright hair was clotted with dirt.

"Kitty? Oh, God, answer me." Splinters dug into his bare feet but he ignored them. He crouched beside her and pulled her hair from her face.

Green eyes blinked up at him and his relief was so great he almost fell over backward. "Jack. What happened?"

"The trapdoor gave way. Are you all right? Does anything hurt? Can you move?"

"Everything. I don't know." She raised herself onto her elbow and attempted to sit up before she cried out in pain. Her face went utterly white.

"What is it?"

"My ankle," she gasped. Jack looked down and saw that her bare left foot was twisted at an unnatural angle.

"You've broken it. What else hurts, sweetheart? Did you hit your head? Can you breathe okay?" His hands flew over her, gently feeling for any other injuries. Her delicate skin was already bruising and swelling around the scrapes on her legs and arms.

"Yes. I mean, I can breathe. I landed on my ankle, I think. I was stepping forward. Look, I'm covered in popcorn." She giggled, sounding a little bit hysterical. "Jack, what are we going to do?"

Satisfied that her ankle was the worst of her injuries, he kissed her forehead and noticed how clammy her skin was. Shock from the fall and the pain.

"Shh. Don't worry, darling. I'm just going to cover you, and then I'll get help."

"How?"

He pulled a dust sheet from one of the covered chairs and tucked it around her, leaving her ankle untouched. It was starting to swell, and there was a sharp lump on one side. "Just stay still, honey. Don't move. Concentrate on breathing slowly. You'll be out of here in no time."

The phone was where he'd left it, under some rags; he thumbed the "on" button. There had to be enough charge left.

One bar. Just enough for a quick call. But no signal.

Jack swore. He'd had enough signal to chat with his dad, but now that Kitty was hurt, now that he needed to get them rescued, it had disappeared? He moved toward Kitty, underneath the trapdoor opening, and almost shouted when a signal appeared. He hit 9-1-1.

"An ambulance. The Delphi Theater, on Congress Street.

She's fallen through a trapdoor and broken her ankle. The door to the theater is broken, you might have to force it open. So maybe the fire department, too. I think she's in shock, please hurry. Jack Taylor. Her name's Kitty Giroux. How long?"

He ended the call and turned toward Kitty. "Hold on darling, it should only be ten—"

The look on her face stopped him short. She had sat bolt upright, and her skin had gone even paler. Her wide eyes stared at him, intensely green and full of pain and betrayal.

They stabbed him through the heart.

"You have a phone," she said. Her voice was quiet, hysteria gone.

He couldn't tear his gaze away from her eyes. He was pinned by them as if by a knife.

"I—"

He'd seen that look before. Ten years ago. Betrayal and pain and soul-wrenching distrust. From those same green eyes.

All their eternal promise gone.

"You had a phone all along," she said.

Jack opened his mouth, but he couldn't speak. His heart was doing something agonizing in his chest.

"You didn't tell me. You trapped me. You used me."

It wasn't an accusation, it was a statement of fact. And her voice wasn't angry. It was resigned. Flat-sounding, without music or warmth.

He found some words, though he knew they weren't good enough before he even spoke them. "Kitty, I didn't—"

"You wanted a good time and you didn't care how I felt." A sob rose in her voice and Jack heard it with a new burst of pain. "It's exactly how you treat all your women. I'm no different."

"That's not true, Kitty, I didn't find the phone until this morning, we'd already made love but I needed to touch you, and then—" His explanation came out in a mad rush, but she closed her eyes, wincing, and he stopped.

He heard her take a deep breath and then she opened her eyes again. "Get some clothes on before the ambulance comes," she said.

"I don't want to leave you."

"Jack. I don't want you near me. Get dressed. Wait by the door for them. Go away."

"Sweetheart—" He reached out his hand for her, and her pale face flushed with anger.

"Do. Not. Touch. Me."

He froze, then slowly brought his hand back to his side.

"I remember you looking like this," he said. It was only just above a whisper. "At the prom. I remember I looked up from kissing Melissa Beauchamp and I saw you, standing there on the dance floor, looking like you're looking at me now."

She didn't say anything. She just looked at him, and the pain in her eyes kept on stabbing him.

"You looked like you expected it. You hoped that I wouldn't, but you expected me to do this. Kitty, you didn't expect it this time too, did you?"

No answer.

"And I remember something else from that night." The words were forcing themselves out of him, hoarse and jagged. "I looked at you and I remember thinking, I hope I never fall in love and hurt that much. And now…" his voice faltered "…I do. You expected me to let you down again."

Kitty closed her eyes. "Please go and get dressed, Jack."

Feeling as if he were leaving his life behind him, he climbed out of the hole and went back to the stage where he'd left his clothes. As he was pulling them on he heard a distant hammering at the front door.

Tugging his sneakers onto bare feet that he only now noticed were smeared with his blood, Jack half hopped, half ran up the aisle. By the time he got to the lobby, the front door was swinging open and he saw a fireman and two paramedics standing in the doorway. The fresh air hit him like cool water. It was dark outside, and he could hear rain.

"She's fallen through the trapdoor," he said. "There's a chair you can step down on."

"What's her name?" the second paramedic asked as the fireman and the first paramedic lowered themselves into the hole.

"Kitty." Helpless, he hovered near the lip of the hole and watched the rescue crew work. They checked Kitty for injuries and stabilized her ankle and got her onto a stretcher. The fireman climbed out of the trapdoor and faced him.

"You own this place?"

"Yes."

"What were you thinking, having an unsound trapdoor?"

"It was safe, but—I opened it. I must not have replaced the cover the right way."

"You were stuck in here?" the fireman asked. "It's a public building. What about the fire escapes?"

"They're locked."

The fireman shook his head in disgust. "Nobody should have been in here without a working fire escape. You could've both been killed."

Every word the fireman said hammered home his opinion of Jack. *Irresponsible jerk.* Guilt twisting in his stomach, Jack could only nod.

"Hey, give us a hand up with this stretcher," called one of the medics. Jack immediately reached down, but after a forbidding look from the fireman he backed away. He watched as they lifted Kitty up to the floor. Her face was drawn with pain, and her eyes were closed.

"Kitty," he pleaded, trying to take her hand in his. She curled her fingers into a tight ball and pulled her fist away.

The paramedics wheeled the stretcher across the lobby and through the vestibule. Jack followed them. The inner door, from the outside, didn't look damaged at all.

"How did you get in?" he asked the fireman.

"Turned the door handle. Wasn't even locked."

The rain was cold on his bare arms and the street was lit from the blue and red flashing lights of the emergency vehicles. He glanced upward; no stars.

The sky felt vast and empty above him.

Jack tried to climb into the back of the ambulance alongside the stretcher but Kitty opened her eyes as he stepped up. "No," she said. Her face was wet, but Jack couldn't tell if she'd been crying or if it was the rain. "Leave me alone."

The paramedic with her shrugged, and Jack stepped back onto the sidewalk. He watched the fireman shut the door, and saw the ambulance pull away.

"Thank you," he said to the fireman.

Jack went back inside the cinema and wheeled his bike out from the lobby. Then he got on it and pedalled as hard as he could toward the hospital. He caught up with the ambulance after a block and a half and followed it all the way.

They took her straight through into the emergency room and wouldn't let him get past Reception without her permission. Jack, soaked with rain and sweat, stood in the middle of the waiting room.

A few of the less obviously sick people regarded him with curiosity. Jack pushed his wet hair back from his forehead and paced. His sneakers squelched and he left puddly footprints on the linoleum floor.

Out of the corner of his eye he caught a glimpse of red hair. Instantly he was searching it out, but it wasn't Kitty. This woman was in a nurse's uniform, and her hair was browner, more auburn than red. He recognized her, though.

"Treena!" he called, and rushed over to her.

His ex-lover looked him up and down. "Hi, Jack. You look like a drowned rat."

Rat was a good description of how he felt.

"Listen, can you do me a favour? There's a woman who's just been admitted, Katherine Giroux Clifford, she's got a broken ankle, she came in an ambulance. Can you see how she is? I need to know if she's okay."

Treena looked him up and down again. She lifted her eyebrows. "Sure," she said and walked off.

Jack felt as if he'd paced five miles before she came back. He nearly leapt on her. "How is she?"

"She's fine. She's got a lot of cuts and bruises and a nasty break in her ankle, but nothing serious. She's gone to X-ray."

"Thank you." He collapsed into the nearest chair and finally felt as if he could start to catch his breath.

When he looked up, Treena was still standing watching him. "I heard this rumor that you gave up sex for a year."

"That's right."

"Do you mind me asking why?"

"Kitty. The woman you just checked on. I was waiting for her."

Treena nodded slowly. "I always knew that when you fell for a woman, you'd fall hard. How's love treating you, Jack?"

"I'm more miserable than I've ever been in my life," he told her truthfully.

She nodded again. "I thought so. When I walked into the room and said you wanted to know how she was, she freaked out. She said I was welcome to you if I wanted you."

Misery swamped him even more. Jack remembered the last time he'd seen Treena, outside the restaurant he'd taken Kitty to. How angry Kitty had been at seeing three of his ex-girlfriends in one night.

He'd asked the wrong person to go check on her. Yet another thing to add to his list of mistakes.

He sighed. "How's it going with your new boyfriend?"

"Fiancé. He's showing promise." Treena checked her watch. "I've got to get back to work. Listen, Jack, you might as well go home. It's late. She doesn't want to see you, and they've called her mother. She'll be okay. You can't do anything. Go get warm and dry."

He stood. Treena was right. If Kitty didn't want him, there was nothing he could do about anything.

His shoulders slumped. "Okay. Thanks. Bye."

Jack went back outside into the rain and got back on his bike to ride home. Maybe the rain would wash away some of this hurt.

Yeah. Right. And he was Gene Kelly.

Jack sat and looked at the darkness.

It wasn't as dark as the Delphi got with the lights out. It definitely wasn't as dark as he felt right now.

But it would do.

Working by touch rather than by sight, he found the bottle opener and pulled a bottle of beer from the six-pack he'd brought. He uncapped the bottle and took a lukewarm mouthful.

There was a sound outside the shut door, and then it opened and let in the semi-light from the front porch.

"Hi, Oz."

Oz's tall silhouette, holding a suitcase and a laptop, stood in the doorway. "Jack? What are you doing in my living room?"

"I was waiting for you to get home from Canada. Your sister let me in on her way out."

Oz put down his bags and snapped on the light. "Why were you waiting in the dark?'

"I like the dark." Jack took another swig of beer.

Oz considered Jack, his eyes narrowed. Then he shrugged, and sat on the worn armchair across from the sofa where Jack was slouching. "Did you have a nice weekend?"

"You could say that. I got trapped in the Delphi with Kitty for thirty hours."

"Hmm. Is that a good thing?"

"That depends how you define 'good'. On the plus side, I've

fallen completely in love with her. On the minus side, she really hates my guts."

"That does seem to be pretty evenly balanced." Oz didn't bother with the bottle opener; he knocked the cap off his beer on the scarred coffee table. He took a long swallow. "Uh, I can't think of any tactful way of saying this, so I'm just going to ask. Are these the beers you promised to buy me for every condom you used?"

Jack gestured at the beer he held. "I owe you one more for this one I'm drinking."

Oz was clearly doing the math. "That's not bad for less than two days."

Jack buried his head in his hands. "Oz, she is the most amazing woman on the face of the earth. I love her. I didn't know it at first, because I'd never been in love before. I thought it was sex. But it's so much more than that. She makes me feel things in ways I didn't even know existed. Whenever I'm near her I never want to let her go. It's like when she's around the world is..." He breathed deep. "It's just better. And I have totally blown it because I am an idiot."

"In what particular way are you an idiot?"

"She'd told me she only wanted to have an affair with me while we were in the Delphi, and that when we were rescued it would be over. Then I found my cell phone in the basement."

"Let me guess. You didn't tell her about it because you didn't want your affair to end."

Jack lifted his head. "I tried to convince her that it didn't have to end. I think I nearly did. But then she found out about the phone."

Oz nodded. "Well, in my opinion most men would have done exactly the same thing. But that doesn't stop it from being a stupid thing to do. Especially if you want a woman to trust you."

"I know. And then she fell through the trapdoor and broke her ankle and it's my fault because I didn't replace the door correctly." Jack drained his bottle of beer. "That's not what's bothering me the most, though."

"What's bothering you the most?"

Jack grimaced. "Do they teach you to parrot questions back in psychology school?"

"Yes. On the first day. What's bothering you the most?"

"Her eyes."

Oz's gaze flicked to the six-pack. "You sure you've only had one beer?"

"It was when she saw I had the phone. She looked at me in this way like I'd betrayed her, like I'd slapped her in the face. But like she was expecting me to. And you know what? She was right. Because I realized something."

"Realized what?"

"That I've been avoiding relationships all my life because when I dumped Kitty on prom night, I saw how horrible love can make you feel. I thought I was trying not to hurt other women. But really I was trying not to get hurt myself. I've taken the easy way out since then. I've never wanted to try anything I might fail at."

Oz nodded slowly. "When you were a teenager, you saw the devastating effects that love can have on somebody and so you decided never to make yourself vulnerable to love. As time went on, you probably had other experiences that reinforced the decision you'd made. For the next ten years you kept all of your relationships with women purely sexual." He opened two more beers and handed one to Jack. "And the movies?"

"The movies were an escape from real emotion. Two hours of no-hassle fun where the problems are always solved. I get it now."

"Then you had a dream about the same person who made you decide to avoid love in the first place."

"My dream was a prediction because I have a psychic grandmother," Jack said.

"I don't believe that rubbish. Dreams are your mind's way of telling you things. Your dream was clearly your unconscious mind telling you that you were ready to reconsider this decision never to fall in love. Kitty was a symbol of love to you, because of your history."

"But she's not a symbol. She's a real woman. I love her. And I'm a jerk."

"Well, that's true, too." Oz got his analytical look. "I wonder if your subconscious knew that Kitty was the woman you could love, or if it was a coincidence."

Jack threw himself back onto the couch. "Oz, this is all far too complicated for me. All I know is that I didn't want to fall in love because I saw Kitty get hurt. Maybe I cared about her even then and I didn't let myself see it. And now I'm completely in love with Kitty and I feel even worse because I hurt her again."

"That's what I said. Except I made sense."

"Whatever. The thing is, I feel terrible. I've never felt worse in my entire life. So I think I've made a mistake."

"I don't follow you," Oz said.

"I shouldn't have listened to my dream. I shouldn't have tried to change my life. It didn't work." Jack downed half his beer in one gulp. "So come on, we're going out."

"What for?"

"I'm going to do what I should have been doing for the past year. We're going to go to a bar, and I'm going to find a woman, and take her home, and have uncomplicated, meaningless sex, and in the morning I'm not going to feel guilty at all." He drank the rest of the beer and slammed the empty bottle down on Oz's table. "In fact, I'm going to feel great. Come on, let's go."

Oz studied Jack. "I'll call a taxi," he said.

As soon as they walked through the door of the bar, Jack spotted two women sitting on their own at a table. "Over there. I'll take the brunette, you can have the blonde."

"Are you sure?" Oz asked. "Don't you want to play it cool for a little while first? Have a drink, check out the talent?"

"What's the point? I wasted a year waiting for Kitty, and I lost her. I'm through with waiting for things. Are you coming, or what?"

"You're the boss," Oz replied mildly, and followed Jack to the table.

"Hi." Jack put on his best dazzling smile. "Do you two mind if we share your table?"

"Not at all." The brunette smiled back at him, and licked her bottom lip. She was busty, wearing a clingy top as well as tight jeans that outlined every curve. Perfect.

"I'm Jack and this is Oz. Can we buy you a drink?"

"I'm Amelia," said the brunette, "and this is Heidi. We'd love two more tequila sunrises, thanks."

"Great." Jack waylaid a waitress, gave her their order, and then sat down next to Amelia. He pulled his chair closer to hers. "So do you have any plans for the evening, Amelia?"

This was going great. Amelia was giving him all the right signals: appraising looks at his body, major eye contact. He was close enough to smell her perfume. It was flowery, not like what Kitty wore. He closed his eyes anyway and tried to detect a warm vanilla note, rich and vivid like the color of Kitty's hair, creamy like her skin.

He opened his eyes. *Stop it.*

"I'm sorry. What did you say you did for a living?" he asked.

She tossed her dark hair over her shoulder before she answered him, and though he heard her speaking, he didn't catch the meaning of what she said. He was feeling that pain inside him again, and the only words he could understand were the ones pulsing inside his head and heart.

I don't want to be here.

The waitress put his beer down in front of him. Jack wrapped his hand around it in a death grip.

Yeah, you don't want to be here, he said to himself. *Tough. Work through it. Charm the pants off of Amelia, and get your old life back.*

He gulped his beer like a man dying of thirst, and then wiped his mouth with the back of his hand and smiled at Amelia.

"That must be interesting," he said, though he had no idea what she'd just said about her job. He forced himself to look into her eyes. They were gray. That probably suited his mood better than Kitty's vibrant summer-green eyes. He felt gray. "You look familiar to me, somehow, Amelia."

"You've probably seen one of my TV commercials."

"Oh!" he said, surprised. "You're an actress?"

She gave him a weird look and nodded slowly. "Um, yeah, that's what I just told you."

"Hey, that's great. That's totally great. I love actresses."

An actress. Perfect. Really, just—perfect. He tried to picture kissing Amelia's wide red mouth.

All he could see was two silhouettes, embracing on the silver screen. All he could taste was the pink sweetness of Kitty's lips.

He swigged his beer again. It didn't quite erase the remembered taste from his mouth, so he drank the rest of it and signalled for another one.

"What do you like best about being an actress?" He trained all his effort and concentration on Amelia. She was sexy, she was nice, she was an actress. He was going to forget about Kitty, once and for all.

"Oh, I don't know," Amelia answered. "It's not the hours, because you're either working all the time or not at all. And it's certainly not the money." She trailed her fingers around the rim of her cocktail glass. "I guess it's just because it's what I've always wanted to do. It's my dream."

Jack stood up quickly enough to send his chair toppling over behind him.

"I'm sorry, Amelia. I've got to go."

Amelia, Oz and the blonde were all looking at him. Amelia and the blonde had their mouths open in surprise. "Oz?" Jack said, his voice strangled.

"Yeah, buddy." Oz stood up and put some bills on the table for the drinks. "Nice to meet you both, Heidi, Amelia. Have a good evening."

As soon as they got outside Jack went to the first tree he saw and kicked it. "Don't say it, Oz. I don't think I can handle any psychological truths right now."

Oz put his hand on his shoulder. "I can't say anything you don't know already, Jack. For once. Come on, let's go home and see if we can find some knee pads. I think you might have to do some begging to get Kitty back."

CHAPTER THIRTEEN

"WELL, that's one thing I can say about the Giroux family. They always were quick healers. One time your dad shot himself in the foot and he was back out hunting by the next weekend. You and Nick take after him that way. The healing, not the hunting. Thank God."

If I heal so quick, why do I feel so terrible? Kitty thought. She glanced at her mother in the driver's seat of her creaky Subaru. Sue had been relentlessly cheerful throughout the doctor's visit for a new cast on Kitty's ankle. It was driving her crazy. Like the insistent itching underneath her cast, only worse.

"I still don't think you're well enough to drive all the way to New York, though," her mother continued.

"The Mercedes is an automatic. I'll be fine."

"You should be resting your ankle. Driving isn't resting."

"Mom, I'll be fine."

"I don't understand why you want to take that job in New York. It's working for someone else, isn't it? You were so excited to set up your own business when you came here, and now you're giving up."

"I'm not giving up. I don't have a choice. Without the Delphi job, I don't have any work. I can't run a business without any work."

As soon as she'd got out of the emergency room she'd

e-mailed one of her former colleagues and asked for a job at his new firm in New York. And when he'd said he could give her work, though only on a temporary basis at first and only helping on other designers' projects, she'd accepted it right away.

Almost right away. She'd hesitated for a minute, listening to her heart that cried out in agony at the thought of leaving Portland and Jack behind. At failing once again. But that agony was hopeless, and if she stayed here it was only going to get worse.

Especially if she had to keep hiding every time Jack came to the house.

Her mother stopped the car at a light and turned to face Kitty. "You do have work. The Delphi job is still yours. Or have you forgotten that Jack Taylor has phoned and come by the house several times every day for the past week to beg you to take it?"

"I'm not going to work on the Delphi." Kitty stared resolutely at the red light. She wished her mother would go back to being annoyingly cheerful.

"Obviously, as you haven't answered the phone or talked with Jack. But I have, and even I can tell that it's not just the job he's begging you to take. That man is crazy in love with you."

"That man is crazy in *lust* with me. There's a very big difference."

Sue continued on as if she hadn't heard. "And from the way you've been behaving, like a bear with a headache, you feel something for him, too. I'm getting fed up with you hiding all the time. Why don't you face it?"

"The light is green."

Her mother snorted in exasperation. The Subaru jerked forward, and Kitty looked away from the traffic light and saw where they were. She sat bolt upright in panic.

"Turn left! Mom, go left here!"

"Why? It's easier to go down Congress Street." They went straight through the intersection.

"I don't want to see the Delphi." Her heart was hammering nearly hard enough to shake the car. She took a shaky breath and closed her eyes.

The car swerved and then stopped. Kitty opened her eyes and saw that her mother had pulled over to the curb and was looking at her with fierce concern and exasperation.

"What *do* you want, Kitty?"

"I want this job in New York."

"I don't believe you."

Kitty threw her head back against the seat in frustration.

"Mom. I can't have what I want. I want my own business, yes. But I can't afford to do that right now, with no work and no contacts. I'll go to New York and save some money and do some more planning and then I'll start again."

"And Jack? Do you want him, too?"

Kitty drew in a shaky breath. She would not cry. She was not going to be hurt by this. Not permanently. Girouxs were quick healers. It had been a whole week since they'd been rescued, and she hadn't cried yet, and she was not going to do it now.

"Yes. I do." Her voice caught on the words, and she took a moment to swallow back her tears. "But it would never work out. Jack's not the type to commit to one woman. He admits himself that he doesn't know what love is. He thinks he wants me now, but it won't last long."

"You could've fooled me. In my experience a man doesn't buy that many flowers unless he means it. Our garbage cans are full of them."

"Mom, trust me. The man has made a lifetime career out of charming women. I bet he has an account at the florists'."

Her mother shook her head stubbornly. "I've seen his face. He's desperate."

"Desperate to get laid. He lied to me. Don't be shocked by this, but he lied to me so that he could sleep with me. It was just my stupid, rotten luck that I fell in love with him." She choked on the words.

Her mother smoothed Kitty's hair back and tucked it behind her ear, and that gesture was so simple, so tender, so like how Jack had touched her when she'd foolishly confessed her failures to him, that the tears climbed over her defences and spilled out of her eyes.

"Oh, honey," Sue said. She unbuckled her seat belt and scooted over to wrap her arms around Kitty. Kitty relaxed into this love that had never failed her and let her tears fall onto her mother's soft cotton jacket. "I'm sorry that he lied to you."

Kitty wiped her tears away, though it didn't work because they kept on coming—big, wet tears that came without sobs just swelled from her eyes and fell down her cheeks.

"It's the same as it's always been, Mom. I'm a failure in love, like I am with everything else. I fell in love with Jack in high school and he dumped me at the prom. I married Sam and he left me for his first wife. And now I'm in love with Jack again and it's no good because I can't trust him." She sniffed. "Just stinking awful luck."

Sue gave her another hug, and then reached in the glove compartment and pulled out a packet of tissues. "I don't want to upset you, honey. But luck doesn't work like that. Not with you, not with anybody."

"Of course it does. Look at me now. We've just had to go to the doctor to get a brand-new cast because I got the old one wet. Bad luck."

"No, it's not bad luck. You got the old cast wet because you were stubborn and tried taking a bath with your ankle up on the side of the tub, and it fell in. It's like Sam. You decided to marry him because you cared about him, but you didn't love him, not really. So it wasn't surprising it didn't work out. We make our own luck, Kitty. We make our own success. I know that some bad things have happened to you, but that happens to all of us. What counts is what we do when those things happen."

Kitty gave her nose an undignified blow. The tears were still dropping, but not quite as fast now. "That's a nice idea, but—"

"It's true. Take me, for example. If I'd been afraid of failure when I was left with you two kids and no husband and no money, where would we be now? I made my own luck. And it worked out okay. More than okay."

"But he still left you, Mom. He never came back." Kitty swallowed hard. "It doesn't matter how many times Jack tries to apologize to me. He can't be trusted. He'll leave. Like Dad did."

Sue shook her head. "If your father had been the type of man who could bear to apologize, he never would've left in the first place."

She put the car into gear and pulled out from the curb. Kitty watched her mother as she drove. She wore a ten-year-old jacket and twelve-dollar jeans and she was the bravest woman Kitty had ever met.

Sue suddenly twisted the steering wheel. The Subaru swerved and screeched to an abrupt halt again, throwing Kitty forward against her seat belt. Her cast knocked against the side of the car. Kitty heard a squeal of brakes behind them and a blaring horn.

"What's wrong?"

"Kitty," said Sue, pointing out the windshield, "I know you don't want to see the Delphi, but I think you should look at this."

Kitty leaned forward and looked at the Delphi, which was just in front of them. It looked the same. Beautiful, graceful, windowless, with its heavy outer doors closed.

Then she saw the marquee over the entrance, where the names of the movies would be advertised in foot-high black letters on the illuminated white background. And saw what was spelled out there, in big black capitals, for all of Portland, Maine, to see.

JACK TAYLOR LOVES KITTY GIROUX.

The tears stopped leaking from her eyes. In fact, everything stopped. Kitty stopped breathing, the traffic halted around them, the world stopped turning, and she stared at the sentence hanging in the air in front of her.

Oh, my God.

Did he?

For a brief moment, while the question hung in her mind, anything was possible.

Then the truck behind them honked its horn again and the world started up. And with it, her common sense. Real life wasn't like a movie. No matter how much she wanted it to be.

"Let's go, Mom." Her voice sounded tinny, flat to her own ears.

"Kitty, this doesn't look like the work of a man who doesn't know what love is."

Kitty put down the damp tissue she'd been holding. She'd stopped crying. In fact, she didn't feel very much of anything at all.

"It looks like the work of a man who thinks he knows what he's doing," she said. "But he doesn't. Jack's the type of man who does what he feels like without thinking about the implications. He bought a popcorn machine and a year's worth of Raisinets before he'd even finished half the renovations. He had a cell phone hidden the entire time we were trapped in the Delphi."

She took a deep breath, and let it out slowly. "Jack might think he's in love with me. But he isn't. It won't last long. Can we go now? I need to finish packing."

Stop. Scroll back to beginning. Play again.

Kitty sat on her narrow bed and watched the moving pictures.

Red velvet seats, row after row facing her like a mute audience. Gilded fruit ascending the walls, supporting an infinite canopy of stars. A golden proscenium framing a silver screen that waited for shadows to be cast onto it. And full circle, standing half smiling in indigo jeans and white T-shirt, about to kiss her for the second time in ten years: Jack.

It only lasted a few seconds. This time Kitty clicked the back button on her laptop's video player and watched the images reverse, from Jack to the screen to the stars to the seats. Then hit play again.

She wished she'd left the camera running. Caught the next few minutes when he'd touched her, pressed his lips to hers. Then she could have had that forever, too.

Not that she needed a film of his kiss to remember every little thing about how it had felt and tasted. And to feel the pain at knowing that she'd never taste it again. But she couldn't help looking at the film over and over again, like probing a sore tooth with her tongue. Feeling the loss wasn't too bad, because it distracted her for a moment from what her mother had said.

Her numbness after seeing Jack's message had lasted all of about fifteen minutes. Then had come the crashing, crushing realization that her mother had been absolutely right about two things.

There was no such thing as bad luck.

And, right now, Jack Taylor really did love her.

"That should make me happy," she said to the picture of Jack on the screen. "But it doesn't. Why?"

The picture held no answers, but she could supply them herself. If there was no such thing as bad luck, then all of the failures in her life had been because of one thing.

Herself. Not being good enough. All the missed chances, all the times coming second best. They had all been her own fault.

She hadn't been good enough to keep Sam, and she hadn't even loved him. How on earth could she hope to keep Jack when he was better than Sam in every way? How could she ever compete with the dozens of women who breezed in and out of

Jack's life? They were everywhere. In restaurants, on the sidewalks, in the damn emergency room, for God's sake.

She'd never be exciting enough or beautiful enough or sexy enough for Jack. Not now that they were outside and he could have anybody that he wanted.

Now that she was being truthful to herself, she could admit that she'd known that all along. Blaming Jack for lying to her was just an excuse. Of course he'd lied to her. She'd told him she wouldn't have sex with him after they were rescued. He liked having sex with her, so he didn't want to get rescued. It was a totally normal male thing to do.

But by blaming him for making a mistake, she didn't have to face up to the probability that if Jack's love wasn't real, it would only be one person's fault.

Hers.

Downstairs, she heard the back door open and shut and she heard her mother talking. She couldn't help it. She was drawn to the idea of Jack like one of her mom's magnets to her refrigerator. She hopped out into the hallway and to the top of the stairs, where she leaned most of her weight on her uninjured leg and listened.

"Those are beautiful flowers," her mother was saying. "Shame they're going in the garbage can. Here, have a seat and I'll try to get her to come down. I don't think she will, though. She's got it in her head that she never wants to see you again."

"I know." Jack's voice made her heart speed up. "I never thought I'd say this, but I'm beginning to suspect I'm not very good with women." Her mother laughed.

"She's stubborn," Sue said. "Like her father."

I am not like my father, she thought. *I can apologize. I don't leave.*

She remembered her half-packed bags.

"Anyway," Jack continued, "I really need to talk with her.

Do you think maybe I should write a letter, or do you think she'd tear it up?"

Kitty thought about the message he had left her, on the Delphi's marquee. Big and bold, a foot-high statement of what he wanted. It was real, she was convinced of it now. She just wished she could be convinced that it would last.

I could try. The thought burst out suddenly, like a small but noisy firecracker in her brain. *Maybe this time I won't fail.*

"How's her ankle?"

"She had a new cast put on today. The doctor says she's doing fine. The Girouxs were always fast healers."

Right. She had to do something quick, before her mother told Jack that story about her father shooting himself in the foot and embarrassed her forever. She called down the stairs. "Jack?"

She heard footsteps approaching the bottom of the stairs, and then Jack's voice. "Kitty?"

"I can't get down the stairs that well. Can you come up?"

He ran. And ended up on the next-to-top step, about two inches away from her, his brown eyes and expressive face level with hers.

"Hi," he said.

She could feel his breath on her cheek. And his smell, woodsy aftershave, mingled with more. The scent of himself, the scent she'd learned by breathing it with every breath while they'd been in the Delphi. Her heartbeat sped up and she felt slightly dizzy.

"Hi," she said.

"How are you?"

"I'm okay."

The words couldn't describe a hundredth part of how she felt. Hot, cold. Pierced by a joy that was almost pain at seeing him again.

Her mother's voice called up from the kitchen. "Kitty! Jack!

I'm going out for a while, see you later! I'll probably be gone a really long time!" The back door slammed.

"I really like your mother," Jack said.

"She's not exactly subtle," Kitty replied.

For a moment they just looked at each other.

Jack bit his lip, and then suddenly he was talking, fluently and fast, every word a bolt of energy. "Kitty, I'm so sorry I didn't tell you about the phone. I was really, really wrong and I don't blame you for being mad at me."

She knew already, but she wanted to hear him say it. "Why didn't you tell me?"

"I wanted to convince you to give our relationship a chance first. I didn't want to lose you."

"Not being honest with somebody is a pretty good way to lose them."

"I know that now. I knew it then, too, but I was too wrapped up in what was going on to think it through." Jack raised his hands, palms up. "What can I say? I made a mistake and I'm really sorry about it. I told you, I have a lot to learn about love."

That word made her stomach do a little skip and her heart thrum even harder.

He really meant it, didn't he?

"So do I," she said.

There were two inches between them. It felt like a lot less. The warmth from Jack's body caressed her. And, as always, his eyes made her feel as if she were melting into a pool of chocolate. The word "love" hung between them in the air.

"Kitty, I—"

Jack broke the silence and her leg chose exactly that moment to wobble. He reached out and steadied her with a hand on either arm. "You shouldn't be standing on that ankle," he said, and scooped her up into his arms.

It had felt as if they were touching anyway, but nothing

could have prepared Kitty for the rush of sensation when he picked her up and cradled her to his chest. She gasped and curled her arms around his neck, feeling her cheek close to his and feeling protectiveness in his gentle hands.

"Where's your bedroom?"

Kitty pointed with her good foot. She couldn't quite breathe, so speaking was out of the question.

He carried her into her tiny Madonna-strewn bedroom and stood in front of her bed, making no move to put her down. He turned his face into her hair and inhaled deeply. "I've missed touching you," he murmured.

Back in the heaven of Jack's arms. The place where she felt the safest, even though a corner of her mind was still telling her it was far too good to be true.

Kitty twined her fingers in Jack's silky hair and imagined the sweet oblivion of tumbling onto her bed and making love with Jack again. It would only take a single movement of her face toward his, could begin with a single kiss.

She felt his arms and body stiffen, his fingers suddenly digging into her thighs and ribs. She followed his gaze to the corner where her half-packed suitcase sat.

"You're leaving."

"I—" She had to swallow and start again, because his grasp and the obvious pain in his face had stolen her breath again. "I've accepted a job in New York."

"But I need you for the Delphi. I need you for me, Kitty."

And then what she'd decided not to do was happening, and Jack had pulled her even closer to him and had captured her mouth with his and was kissing her and she was lost.

She'd missed him so much. Until this moment, she hadn't even known the extent of it. With a sigh in her throat she opened her lips to him. His tongue met hers and plunged inside her mouth as if he were starving for her.

With this part of him inside her, Kitty suddenly wanted it

all. Every inch of his skin pressed against hers, the full length of him buried inside her, his eyes burning into hers as they had in the Delphi.

Kitty pulled her face away from his. "Stop," she gasped.

"Why?" Jack's voice was hoarse. "Kitty, please stay. I'm dying for you, here."

She believed it. His eyes were full of the starkest hunger she'd ever seen. She knew she looked the same way.

But she needed more. If she was going to turn her back on the safe bet in New York, if she was going to trust to her own luck and hope and Jack, she needed more than just desire.

She needed to know if she was good enough to keep his love.

"I can't have sex with you," she said. "Not right now."

It was like all the ardor, all the life in Jack's face just vanished. "I see." He set her down on her bed. "I've blown it, haven't I? You're going to New York."

"No." She missed him immediately, and she reached out and caught his hand before he could step back. "I mean, yes, I plan to go to New York. If that's my only choice. But—" her voice wavered, and then strengthened as she spoke the words aloud at last "—I'd much rather stay here with you."

"But you're not sure if you can," he said. "You don't know if you can trust me. You think I'm going to change my mind and betray you again. I won't, Kitty. I can't. There isn't any other woman in the world for me."

"I saw what you put on the marquee of the Delphi," she said.

His face gained back a little of its life. "I couldn't think of a single movie that was better than the truth."

"I need to know that it is the truth. I can't settle for a whim or an affair. I can't be just the latest woman in Jack Taylor's life. Do you understand what I mean, Jack?"

He sat beside her on the edge of the bed. It was a tiny single bed, and her thigh pressed against his. "I've never felt this way about any woman before. Nothing even close, Kitty. They were friends, they were fun. You, you're everything I ever wanted and a lot of things I never even knew I wanted until I met you. I didn't even know what love was until I fell in love with you. And I fell in love with you the minute I saw you again. Probably even before."

"Before?"

Jack took a deep breath. "Okay, this is going to sound crazy. Nobody knows about it except for Oz, and he only believes me because he's a psychologist who's worked with criminals and insane people and he knows the weird workings of the human mind. But it's true, I swear."

"What?"

"Just over a year ago, I had a dream. About you. We were making love."

"But you didn't even know me a year ago. I mean, you did, but we hadn't seen each other since we were teenagers."

"I know. But it was you. I didn't know who it was at the time, though. All I knew was that it was the most incredible thing I'd ever experienced. So I decided to give up having sex with anybody until I found the woman in my dream."

"Me?" His hand in hers was suddenly more than wonderful. It was wondrous, it was absolutely unbelievable.

"You. I knew it as soon as I saw your eyes when you came to the Delphi. And when we made love, though it wasn't the same as my dream, it was so much like it that I knew I'd been right. That was why I couldn't tell you about the phone, Kitty. My dream was coming true, and I couldn't let it go."

Kitty stared at Jack. "And how long did you go without sex for?"

"Eleven months before I saw you. Over a year before we made love. God, it was worth it."

"Are you telling me that you were faithful to me for eleven months, Jack, before you even knew who I was?"

"Yes."

"You'd been split up with all of those women for nearly a year when I met you again?"

"Yes."

"And all this time you were, like, turning down dates?"

"I had to get an unlisted phone number."

Kitty's mouth was hanging open. She shut it, and stared at Jack.

"Of course at the time I thought I was waiting for the best sex in the world. And I was, but I was waiting for love, too. I was just too dumb to know it."

She could only just barely speak. "I don't think you're dumb."

"Oh, no, I was dumb. I tried all my normal things on you; I tried to charm you and it wasn't working and I was desperate. But until we got stuck in the Delphi you didn't trust me, and you don't trust me now."

"I want to trust you," she said.

Jack reached into the pocket inside his coat and took out a battered roll of paper. "Your mother said you threw away all the flowers I sent you, so I brought you something else instead." He handed the paper to her.

She had to take her hand from his to unroll the paper. It was the drawing she'd done of him in the Delphi. She remembered how fiercely she'd wanted to do it, to capture something of Jack for herself.

"I've been carrying this around since we got rescued," he said. "It felt like part of you that I could still hold. This drawing is amazing, Kitty, and so was our time together. You opened up to me and let me share your life. You helped me see myself; you helped me know who I am. In a big way you made me who I am, probably more than you'll ever know. Even I am not dumb enough to let you go. Unless you make me."

Jack cupped her face in his hand and tenderly stroked his thumb over her lips. "I've been trying for days to think of how I can prove to you that I can be trusted. That I really want to commit myself to you. That I'll love you forever. But I can't think of any way to prove all that. Except for being with you and loving you forever. If you'll let me."

This time Kitty really was speechless. She looked at Jack. His face was so intent, watching her. She could feel every muscle in his body tense as he waited for her answer. He bit his bottom lip, looking vulnerable and eager, full of energy and passion.

He was what she really wanted, more than anything else in the world. And she was more than just good enough for him. He'd waited for her when he didn't know who she was. He'd looked for her. He'd kept a part of her inside his jacket, close to his heart, when he couldn't see her. He wanted her more than anything else, too.

So she took a deep breath and she said the words that she'd been dying to say to Jack Taylor for nearly half her lifetime.

"I love you, Jack. I've loved you since the moment I saw you in the lunch line thirteen years ago. I fell in love with you all over again in the Delphi, and I couldn't tell you because I was too scared. But I'm not scared anymore. I love you. I've never loved anybody but you. I'll never stop loving you."

And she reached for him and brought his face to hers and kissed him with all of the love and desire and happiness she felt. Jack groaned and they sank to lie facing each other on the narrow bed.

"Does this mean you'll stay?" he asked.

"I'll stay."

"And you'll try to trust me?"

"I already do."

"I love you, Kitty."

His kiss this time was so passionate that it stole all of her breath, all of her thoughts, everything except for this joy that she felt in being in his arms again, here in this bed where she'd wished and prayed that she could have him.

"How do you make love to someone with a broken ankle?" he asked, dropping hot kisses on her face and neck.

"Carefully, I think."

He lifted her sweater over her head and unfastened her bra with nimble, reverent fingers. He paused only to brush a thrilling kiss on the swell of both of her breasts, and then he was untying the drawstring of her sweatpants and drawing them down. He looked up at her with one eyebrow cocked.

"No underwear?"

"*You* try to get a pair of panties over an enormous cast."

"I might just try that. Later." He eased her sweatpants over her foot and, exquisitely gently, over her cast. And then he looked at her, and, as always, Kitty felt his eyes as if he were touching her, all over, more wonderfully than anyone but him had ever touched her before. She felt precious. Beautiful.

Loved.

Jack stood, and she watched him remove his own clothes. She relished every inch of his skin as it was exposed to her sight. First his strong shoulders and chest, the muscles that she was dying to touch again. Then his lean hips and long legs as he kicked off his jeans. Then, as he pulled off his boxers, his glorious arousal, naked, blatant and unashamed, the most obvious sign of his desire for her.

Obvious? It was huge. If he came any closer to the bed it would probably poke her in the eye.

Kitty laughed aloud.

"What? Why am I funny?" He raised one eyebrow.

"I never thought I'd see a gorgeous naked man in my childhood bedroom. I sort of feel like I should cover the stuffed animals' eyes."

"As long as they're our only audience, I don't mind." Jack went to the door and shut it.

How did her heart suddenly feel so light, as if her chest were full of sunshine? She giggled, scooped up a teddy bear from the floor next to the bed, and threw it at him. Jack caught it and with exaggerated care, sat it facing away from them on the bookcase. Then he reached in the pocket of his jacket, lying on the floor.

"I brought something else for you, just in case I got lucky." He held up a small pink packet. "I don't think we got a chance to try the Tutti-Frutti."

She stopped laughing when he lay next to her on the bed and began to touch her, but the glow of happiness still hadn't left her. She couldn't stop smiling. Not even while she was kissing him. He just felt so good.

Jack's hands caressed her body gently, stroking from the hollow of her back up her spine, then around to her waist. He took her breasts in his hands and she gasped as her desire became hot, overwhelming, like the sun on a scorching August day.

"I want you now," she whispered. There would be time to go slowly later. There would be all the time in the world. Right now she needed him joined with her. She needed to have Jack and everything she felt about him surrounding her, penetrating her, moving deep inside her.

"I want you more than I've ever wanted anyone," he said. "Anything."

She reached for him and guided him into her, wrapping her uninjured leg around his lean hip. Oh yes, this was where she belonged. Forever.

Kitty took Jack's hand and brought it to her mouth. She felt his fingers touching her smile as he began to move inside her, so slowly and gently. He drew her hand to his face and made her feel his own smile, nipping at each of her fingers. Carefully, tenderly, he began to move faster.

The sun inside Kitty grew hotter, liquid fire, melting all the pain and frustration she had felt all this week into a delicious pool of ecstasy. And then that pool was spilling over and she felt her body shudder and dissolve.

"Jack!" she cried out, holding onto him as hard as she could, hearing him cry out with his own climax. She looked into his eyes and saw that, to Jack, she was the most beautiful woman in the world.

"That was it," he gasped.

She was already sinking into hazy bliss. "What?" she said.

"That was my dream. That was it exactly. Oh, my God, it came true. It was even better." He grabbed her head in his hands and kissed her.

"You dreamed about making love with me in my mother's house while I had a broken ankle?"

He traced her features with his finger. "Well, not about your mother and your ankle. The love. I dreamed about that. That was why it was so incredible. And I woke up before I could see what happens next."

"What happens next?"

A slow smile spread over his face. "I ask you to marry me."

Kitty kissed Jack Taylor. Her first, and only love.

"You," she said, "have just made all of my dreams come true."

EPILOGUE

"YOU'RE never going to stop being obsessed with sex, are you?"

Jack didn't look up from feeding a steady stream of quarters into the condom machine. "It's my wedding night, Oz. I'm allowed to be obsessed with sex. Besides, this is married sex. I think it's going to be even better than engaged sex." He slotted two more quarters into the machine, and caught the condoms in his other hand. "And engaged sex has been amazing."

Oz was silent for so long that Jack finally glanced over at him. His black tuxedo was very dark against the gleaming white tiles of the Delphi's men's room. He was watching Jack, his face keen and thoughtful.

"You're the happiest man I've ever seen," Oz said.

Jack nodded. "I know."

"You deserve it. You and Kitty have worked hard to make the Delphi what it is. And you love each other." Oz shoved his hands into his pockets. "If you weren't my best friend, I'd be jealous of you."

Jack wasn't observant like Oz. He couldn't watch someone and figure out what they were thinking and what their problems were. But looking at Oz, now, he could see that his best friend was lying.

Oz was jealous. He was just trying to cover it up because he didn't want Jack to feel bad. And Jack would bet everything he owned that Oz had never been jealous of him before, in all their years of friendship.

He clapped Oz on the shoulder. "It'll happen to you, Oz. One day you're going to be minding your own business somewhere and you'll see a woman and you'll know she's the one you want to be with forever, no matter what."

Oz shrugged. "Love grows out of mutual understanding and knowledge. You and Kitty had a formative emotional connection long before you had your dream about her. I don't believe in love at first sight."

"I'll remind you of that someday. Here, I got these for you. A thank-you present for being my best man." Jack gave Oz his handful of condoms. "They'll bring you luck."

Oz laughed, and dropped them into the pocket of his tuxedo jacket. "Thanks. I'll buy you a beer for every one I use."

"So did you come in here to tell me I was obsessed with sex, or did you have some news I didn't already know about?"

"Just that the last of your guests have left, and that I'm going home, too. And that your wife is waiting for you in the back row of the auditorium."

"My wife," Jack repeated as they left the men's room and walked across the gleaming parquet floor of the Delphi's lobby. "Married sex. Wow."

Oz shook his head, smiling, and went out the perfectly oiled vestibule doors, and Jack turned to join Kitty in the Delphi's auditorium.

The lights were still down in the theater when he walked in, and the last of the movie credits were rolling on the screen against a universe of shining stars. He slid into the velvet seat beside Kitty and took her hand. The stars were reflected in her eyes.

"See?" Kitty said. "I told you it was a great idea to watch a movie at the end of the reception."

He squeezed her hand. He could feel the gold band, warm

from her skin, on her third finger. For the thousandth time Jack marvelled at how one woman could be the entire world to him: friend, lover, partner, wife.

"Kitty Giroux Taylor, I believe I've turned you into a movie buff," he said, letting go of her hand and trailing his fingers over the ivory silk of her sleeve. He stroked up her arm, across her shoulder, and down the elegant bodice of her dress. He heard her breath catch when his palm skimmed over her breast.

Jack leaned over the armrest of the red velvet seat and grasped Kitty by her waist. He lifted her up over the armrest and into his lap. Her full skirts made a rich rustling sound as she nestled against him, her bottom a tantalizing pressure on his groin. Her hair smelled of warm vanilla and the white roses that were entwined in it. He breathed deep.

"I'm the luckiest woman in the world," she said.

He kissed her. She tasted sweet, as if she'd been licking candy. But it was just her. Jack let himself be lost in her for a while as the credits rolled on the silver screen in front of them and the movie music played in the vast, empty cinema.

The music ended with a flourish, and they parted. In the flickering light from the projector, the gilded leaves and the silver stars glowed. The velvet curtains were hung with flowers from their wedding ceremony, hours earlier. They'd taken their vows on the stage where, eight months before, Kitty and Jack had made love and discovered that anything was possible.

"Where did you disappear to just now?" she asked, her voice husky and so, so sexy.

"I made a visit to the condom machine. And I talked with Oz. I think he's in shock. He's always been the responsible one who wanted a steady relationship. He's probably trying to figure out how on earth his feckless best friend ended up married before him."

"Maybe we should lock him in the Delphi with someone."

Jack shook his head. "Uh-uh. I'm all for finding a woman for Oz, but the Delphi is ours."

"You're right. It is."

Kitty pulled his head down to hers and kissed him again, threading one hand through the hair at the back of his head and stroking the other up the front of his white linen shirt.

Jack had intended to wait until they'd gotten to the hotel suite he'd booked for their wedding night. But he couldn't help it. Kitty looked stunning in her 1930s-style ivory dress, but she'd look even better out of it.

He slipped his hand up and underneath her skirt and caressed up the length of one long, silk-clad leg. At the top, his fingers met warm naked skin. She was wearing stockings. His hand crept up a little farther, and touched the satin and soft lace of her underwear. Jack could easily imagine the wisp of white barely covering her body.

Forget the hotel suite. They'd made love for the first time in the Delphi, after all. It seemed right to make love here for the first time as husband and wife.

"So," said Kitty, her voice shaky and breathless from what he was doing underneath her dress, "what movie are we going to show at the grand opening next month?"

"We've got a honeymoon to get through before that. A honeymoon I intend to begin right now." Jack's left hand fumbled with the buttons on the back of Kitty's dress. "Why does this darn dress have so many buttons?"

"To teach you the rewards of hard work." Kitty wriggled to let him slide her dress down her shoulders.

"Oh, believe me, I've learned," Jack murmured, kissing the freckle Cassiopeia on her shoulder. "Which movie do you think we should show?"

"I don't care. As long as it has a happy ending." Kitty turned in his arms and faced him. Her smile, as always, nearly knocked him out. "As long as it shows some dreams coming true."

He kissed his wife underneath a hundred silver stars, in a room full of flowers and hope, and knew one thing for certain.

Tonight, Jack Taylor was going to make love with the most beautiful woman in the world.

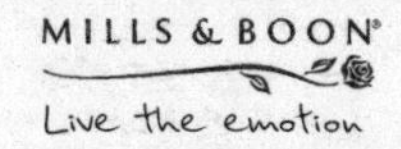

Modern romance™

THE WEDLOCKED WIFE *by Maggie Cox*

Reece Villiers is handsome, incredibly driven, successful – and too proud to show his love. Sorrel has left him, and the only solution can be divorce. Until he realises that she's pregnant! Suddenly Reece is insisting wedlock is the only answer if she is to do the right thing for her baby…

AT THE SPANIARD'S CONVENIENCE
by Margaret Mayo

When Spaniard Lucio Masterton discovers he has a child he knew nothing about, he takes immediate action. And what better way to start than with Kirstie Rivers, the child's mother? Kirstie has been terribly hurt by the billionaire but under the Spanish sun, she finds Lucio hard to resist…

THE ANTONIDES MARRIAGE DEAL
by Anne McAllister

Greek magnate Elias Antonides has single-handedly turned his family's fortunes around – so when he discovers his father has gambled away a vital share he's furious! And he's stuck with a new business partner – stunning heiress Tallie Savas…

IN THE SHEIKH'S ARMS *by Sue Swift*

Cami Elison knew she was playing with fire when she met Sheikh Rayhan ibn-Malik. He had sworn he would make her swindling father pay – by stealing Cami's virginity. But would the Sheikh's lust for revenge turn into love for the innocent beauty he was determined to possess…?

On sale 7th April 2006

Available at WHSmith, Tesco, ASDA, Borders, Eason, Sainsbury's and most bookshops

www.millsandboon.co.uk

HUSH ***by Jo Leigh*** *Do Not Disturb, Book 1*

A hotel for first class sex? That's the buzz in Manhattan on Piper Devon's opulent new boutique hotel, Hush. When Devon family lawyer Trace Winslow checks in to check out the place rumoured to cater solely to the senses, he's guarded. But it isn't long before he's having a few sleepless nights – with Piper.

SLOW RIDE ***by Carrie Alexander***

Lock & Key, Book 3

When Aurora "Rory" Constable and Tucker Schulz are thrown together at a "lock and key" party, the attraction is undeniable. Despite the simmering sexual tension between them, they decide to fight their feelings and just be friends…until they win a weekend together at an exclusive resort. Then it's a slow, sexy ride to some hot nights!

HOT SHEETS ***by Jeanie London***

Falling Inn Bed…Book 1

Laura Granger had had enough of the little flirtation between herself and Dale Emerson. It's long past time that the bad boy made good his sexual innuendos and hit the sheets with her. And to make sure that she gets her satisfaction, Laura has planned a seduction that he can't resist. It's going to be one red-hot week!

GOOD TO BE BAD ***by Debbie Rawlins***

Manhattan biz-whiz Karrie Albright gets the shock of her life when she has to return to her humble hometown beginnings. Handling the deal on behalf of her company reunites her with Rob Philips, a onetime friend and fantasy lover, who still turns her on… But this time she's not going to let him get away!

On sale 7th April 2006

Available at WHSmith, Tesco, ASDA, Borders, Eason, Sainsbury's and most bookshops

www.millsandboon.co.uk